HERO WANTED!

MARK POWERS

BLOOMSBURY
CHILDREN'S BOOKS
LONDON OXFORD NEW YORK NEW DELHI SYDNEY

BLOOMSBURY CHILDREN'S BOOKS
Bloomsbury Publishing Plc
50 Bedford Square, London WC1B 3DP, UK
29 Earlsfort Terrace, Dublin 2, Ireland

BLOOMSBURY, BLOOMSBURY CHILDREN'S BOOKS and the
Diana logo are trademarks of Bloomsbury Publishing Plc

First published in Great Britain in 2024 by Bloomsbury Publishing Plc

A catalogue record for this book is available from the British Library

ISBN: PB: 978-1-5266-4869-3; eBook: 978-1-5266-4868-6; ePDF: 978-1-5266-4867-9

2 4 6 8 10 9 7 5 3 1

Typeset by RefineCatch Limited, Bungay, Suffolk

Printed and bound in Great Britain by CPI Group (UK) Ltd, Croydon CR0 4YY

To find out more about our authors and books visit
www.bloomsbury.com and sign up for our newsletters

To Laura, John, Sam and Ivy.
With thanks to Kate, Zoe, Eleanor and Jo.

An Unhelpful Map of the County of
Brokenshire

Dart-Hagger Tunnel

Thicket of the Bitter Bark

Crackley

Cantankerous Mountain

Screaming Gate

Crumblechester

Field of the
Bubbling Brook

Smashscape

Rat Tail River

Severton

A Castle

Crystal Chasm

Jackdaw's Wood

Crushing

Eagle Rock

A shed

Shimmering Steppes

Sweet Hills

Laughing Meadow

Fiery Pond

1

The Penultimate Grace

Lying awake in bed one night, twelve-year-old Grace Parker heard what sounded like a horse in the front garden: a string of low, powerful snorts followed by a hollow scraping noise that could have been hoofs clacking on the front path. It went on for several minutes.

A horse, she thought as she lay in the darkness, the thick, fluffy duvet pulled up to her chin. *Yeah, right.*

She turned on her side and squinted at the clock. Its luminous display read 00:00. Midnight. *Woop woop!* Hours and hours before she had to get up for school. There was nothing worse than looking at the clock in what you thought was the middle of the night and discovering you had just one minute to go before the alarm went off. She gave an enormous, blissful yawn and rolled on to her back.

Clack, clack went the noise. *Snort. Snort.* Keen to go back to sleep, she tried to ignore it.

Her stomach felt jittery. What was up with that? Too much dessert after dinner tonight, maybe? She and James had fought over the last helping of bread and butter pudding. Grace hadn't even wanted it but she'd enjoyed the look of disappointment on her twin brother's face when she'd scraped the final serving into her bowl. It was first come first served in their house. James knew the rules.

Grace closed her eyes and tried to dream about flying. This rarely worked. Most often, the dream would start out as planned, but just as she was getting the hang of hurtling through the sky, arms outstretched, the scene would change and she would find herself in the school hall having to sit a maths exam she had done zero revision for. Still, it was always worth a try.

There came another noise now.

Whhhheeeeeerrrrhhhhhhhggggghhhhhggghhhh!

Grace's heart drummed. However cosy her bed was, and however tempting the prospect of a flying dream, she couldn't ignore the strange noise any longer. She sat up, threw aside the duvet and stepped out of bed.

Agh!

She fell back on to the mattress, clutching her foot. Something had bitten her. The thought that, *what? A rat? Eww!* – had a made its home under her bed threatened to turn her stomach jitters into a full-on pukefest. Gathering her courage, Grace rolled on to her front and peeped over the edge of the bed. She saw the faint outline of her hairdryer lying on the carpet, the three pins of its electrical plug jutting upwards like the turrets of a tiny castle. She groaned and rubbed her throbbing foot, glad that at least James wasn't around to witness this particular piece of Grace Parker brilliance. He would have given her one of those concerned, frowning looks of his that was supposed to mean *Aw, poor you!* but which Grace knew really meant *Ha ha! What a complete numpty!*

Ever since she could remember, people had been amazed to discover that Grace and James were twins. Sometimes it seemed even to her that no two human beings on the planet could be less alike. James was tall for his age, athletic, with an easy smile that seemed to melt people's hearts, and had a knack for making friends. Grace, by contrast, was on the short side and, according to her PE teacher, Ms Robertson, had 'all the physical agility of a newborn giraffe on roller skates'. Grace also had a temper, which frequently got her into arguments, and she went through friends the way some kids went through pencils. In arguments with James, other people always sided with him, which infuriated her.

Another thing she got angry about regularly was how easy James seemed to find every activity he turned his hand to. He was captain of the school rugby team, played lead guitar in the school band and frequently received top marks in all his subjects. *No big deal*, he would always say after accomplishing something Grace could only dream about. *No big deal!* The phrase made her grind her teeth. What little she had achieved always came as the result of a hard and frustrating struggle. It was all super unfair. And what made things worse was Grace's certainty that James thought her lack of talent was funny. He never actually laughed out loud when she failed a test or knocked her strawberry milk over her dinner, but she could see the sly glint of amusement in his eyes all the same.

With extra care, Grace swung her legs out of the bed, limped lightly to the window, pulled back the curtain and gazed down into the garden. She made a little gasping noise and rubbed her eyes.

The horse she saw nibbling at the neatly trimmed front hedge was as white as the whitest, cleanest, freshest spring snow. Its small sharp ears twitched and the long white mane on its neck rippled in the night breeze, its whole muscular body glowing with vitality. It was, by some way, the most beautiful thing that Grace had ever seen.

Tingling with excitement and curiosity, she fetched her phone from where it lay charging on her bedside table. Without photographic evidence, she knew, no one would ever believe that this magnificent creature had visited her family's ordinary suburban garden. As she was framing the shot with trembling hands, there came a loud thump and her bedroom door flew open.

Grace let out a shriek and spun around to find a squat, menacing figure silhouetted in her bedroom doorway. In the dim light coming from the landing window, she could just make out the figure's shining bronze armour, and on its head, a fierce bronze helmet sculpted into the shape of a scowling face. In one hand, it held a sword, the narrow silvery blade coated with droplets of what looked like fresh blood.

The figure held out its free hand to Grace.

'Is this 18 Marigold Avenue, Flakebury?' it demanded. Its voice was deep, the accent impossible to place.

'Um … yeah?' said Grace.

'And is your name Grace Parker?' There was something eerily familiar about the voice, too. Like the voice of some distant relative she hadn't seen in many years.

Grace's heart froze. She tried to persuade herself

that this was a bad dream, probably brought on by eating too much bread and butter pudding. But the pain in her foot from where she had trodden on the plug, the pounding of her pulse in her ears, and the noticeable chill of the cooler air from the open bedroom door against the hairs on the back of her neck all told her that this was really happening. Here and now.

She nodded mutely.

'Good,' said the figure, 'then I can die,' and collapsed on to the floor of Grace's bedroom, its armour clanking.

Grace dashed forward to help the stricken figure and, grunting with effort, managed to haul the strange visitor on to her bed, surprised at how little they weighed, even with the plates of armour strapped to their body. Despite what they'd said, the figure was still breathing and very much alive.

'Don't move. I'll get help.'

The figure on the bed seized Grace's wrist in a thickly gauntleted hand. 'No. No healers,' it croaked from within its helmet of polished bronze. 'No point. I am beyond the aid of earthly medicine.'

'Why?' asked Grace. 'What happened to you?'

'Treachery!' moaned the figure. 'I was tricked into eating one of Cardinal Axminster's Lingering Death Apples. No mortal can taste this evil fruit and live. My fate, alas, is sealed.'

Grace frowned. 'Lingering Death Apples?'

'A Lingering Death Apple looks as sweet and wholesome as a normal apple,' explained the figure gravely, 'but its surface is swarming with trillions of unimaginably tiny creatures that attack your body from within if you eat it. Thereafter follows a slow and torturous death. Ghastly!'

'So, like germs giving you food poisoning, then?'

'Food *poisoning*?' repeated the figure, as if it had never heard the phrase before. 'Hmm. As if the food I had eaten had been tainted with some variety of poison? Yes. That would be a very good way of putting it.'

'Then I wouldn't stress about it too much,' said Grace. 'It probably won't kill you. I got food poisoning myself once from a dodgy hot dog. You feel awful for a couple of days and you're in and out of the toilet the whole time, but otherwise you should be fine.'

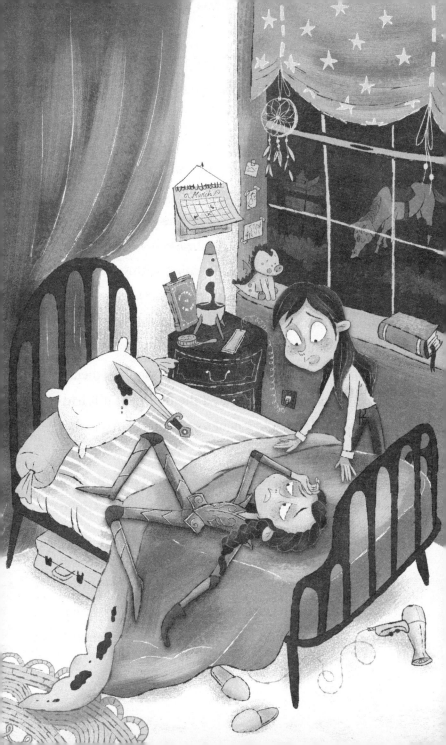

'No!' groaned the figure. 'No one is going to be fine! Don't you see? We are all shortly about to plunged into millennia of agony, misery and chaos!'

Grace grinned and snapped her fingers. 'Hang on. I've just realised what this is! It's cosplay, isn't it? So what are you a character from? And what are you doing here? Did you get lost on your way home from a science fiction convention or something? Or did *he* put you up to this?' She rapped the figure's armour with her knuckles. 'Which of James's friends is in there? Adam? Ross? Yusuf?'

'Your words are but empty fiddle-faddle,' groaned the figure. 'Attend to what I say, I beg you! Woe is upon us! An ancient conflict is nearing its cataclysmic conclusion and in its balance hangs the fate of every living thing. One being alone stands poised on the threshold between the Night of Fear and the Morning of Salvation. That person, Grace Parker, is you!'

'Me?' said Grace. 'Are you absolutely sure you've got the right person? Because people always say I look like this girl in my class, Ava. We have the same pointy chin.'

The figure coughed, gasping for breath, the sound booming from inside the metal helmet. 'You are Grace Parker, are you not?' it enquired impatiently. 'And is not this abode 18 Marigold Avenue, Flakebury?'

'Well, yes, pretty much,' admitted Grace. 'But what's so special about me? I'm just a normal girl.'

'You are the Fifteenth and Last Grace,' said the figure. 'It is your sacred and noble task to lead the People of the Day to victory in the Worthy War.'

'I'm the Fifteenth ... and *last* Grace?'

'*Fifteen Graces protect the Kingdom*,' intoned the figure in a singsong voice, as if recalling a rhyme drilled into it since its earliest schooldays. '*Vanquishing foes in the name of freedom. As one falls, the next replaces. An unbroken chain of Saving Graces.*'

'And what does that mean?'

'It means,' said the figure, removing its helmet, 'that the time has come for you to replace me.'

Grace gasped. The hair may have been styled differently – Grace kept hers long while the armoured figure wore hers in three tight bunches on the top of her head – but otherwise the face of the girl on the bed was identical to Grace's own, even down to the spray of brown freckles on her nose and cheeks. She could have been looking in a mirror.

'Whoa,' said Grace. Her knees were suddenly unable to support her weight. She steadied herself against the bed, mind flailing. Could it really be true? Strange wars in places she had never heard of? Wars she herself was somehow mixed up in?

She gripped the girl on the bed by the shoulders. 'Who *are* you?' she asked.

The girl stared back at Grace through dark brown eyes identical to her own. 'My name is Grace-of-the-Field-of-the-Bubbling-Brook,' she said, her voice less harsh now without the helmet. 'I am the Fourteenth Grace. The Penultimate Grace. After centuries of destruction and death, the Worthy War is about to enter its final, decisive battle. And you, Grace Parker of 18 Marigold Avenue, Flakebury, must be its champion. You must leave this place and journey to Brokenshire, where you will take up the fight on behalf of the People of the Day and finally vanquish the Fearsome Foe.'

Grace gave a nervous laugh. 'This is ridonku-lous, you know. I can't just walk out of here in the middle of the night and go off to join some random war I've never heard of. I have a life. Important things to do. I've just bought a brilliant new pencil sharpener and I can't wait to see how it works out. Can't someone else do it?'

'No!' hissed Grace-of-the-Field-of-the-Bubbling-Brook. 'It must be *you*! You alone are the Fifteenth Grace. The only saviour!'

'But why me?' demanded Grace. 'How did you even get my name and address?'

'From a song!' cried Grace-of-the-Field-of-the-Bubbling-Brook. 'From a song sung by Soros the Sacred Song Singer! His sacred songs record the legends and prophecies of the whole county of Brokenshire. His holy ballads foretold that the Fifteenth Grace would be called Parker and make her home at 18 Marigold Avenue, Flakebury. It was hard work getting to you, Grace Parker, but now I am here to task you with your holy duty. The time has come to take up Swickstipe.'

'Swick —?'

'— stipe, yes.'

With a reverent expression, Grace-of-the-Field-of-the-Bubbling-Brook wiped the blood from her sword on Grace's pillow and offered her the weapon.

Grace tried not to think about what her mum would say about the smears of blood all over her best Egyptian cotton. She eyed the sword warily. 'Whose blood even *is* this, anyway?'

'Cardinal Axminster's,' said Grace-of-the-Field-of-the-Bubbling-Brook. She grinned. 'I got in a few choice thrusts before his Lingering Death Apples took effect! Not enough to dispatch the wicked cleric, however, but never mind that now. This moment is sacrosanct. Take it! Go on! It is your inheritance! Take Swickstipe!'

Grace took the sword. It had a pleasing weight, the metal grip cold and firm in her hand. She marvelled at the way light danced and glimmered along its polished surface. She swished it through the air a few times. It made a splendid *fffsshhewww* noise. She noticed there was an inscription engraved on the metal blade. In thin spidery letters, it read simply, 'Owwwwwwwwwwwwww!'

It suddenly dawned on her that this wasn't a toy.
This was a real soldier's weapon. One that had
almost certainly been used to kill. A terrible shiver
passed through her body and she almost dropped it.
With care she laid the sword down on the bed, as if
fearful it might spring suddenly to life.

'A magnificent bit of kit, is it not?' said Grace-of-
the-Field-of-the-Bubbling-Brook. 'Forged a millen-
nium ago from Hyperion steel in the fires of a sacred
volcano by the master swordsmith Ajax Fandango
himself. Comes in a handy scabbard in a choice of
three attractive colours. I went for walnut. Now
take it and go! Time grows short. Wellingtonia will
explain all as you travel.'

'Welling –?'

'– tonia, yes.'

'Who is –?'

'The horse,' said Grace-of-the-Field-of-the-
Bubbling-Brook.

'Oh! That's your horse outside, is it? Makes
sense, I suppose. Hang on, what do you mean
Wellingtonia will explain? Are you saying your

15

horse can talk? Because that's also ridonkulous.'

Grace-of-the-Field-of-the-Bubbling-Brook seized Grace's wrist again. 'Go now. I mean it. Perhaps I will recover from this "food poisoning", as you call it—'

'Oh, I expect you will,' said Grace.

'Perhaps. Perhaps not. What I do know is that I am currently too unwell to carry out my sacred duty. And therefore, as the prophecy commands, I must hand over to the next Grace to continue. You. Fear not, though, Grace Parker of 18 Marigold Avenue, Flakebury, should I live, I vow I will stay here and take your place as best I can so that your family will not miss you until the day of your victorious return.'

Grace folded her arms. 'So let's get this straight. You're asking me to just walk out of here in the middle of the night and go off to fight some battle in a place I've never heard of while you stay here and pretend to be me?'

Grace-of-the-Field-of-the-Bubbling-Brook nodded gravely. 'Yes. That is precisely what I'm asking.'

Grace gave a snort. 'But why?'

'Why not? What could you possibly have to do that's more important than saving us from misery and ruin?'

Grace suddenly knew why her stomach had been jittery. The memory snapped back into her mind like a stinging elastic band. She cringed.

James's guitar.

A fresh wave of jitters assaulted her stomach.

Oh no, no, no ... !

She hadn't meant to do it. It had been an accident. A terrible, terrible accident.

Following the bread and butter pudding incident, she and James had argued. Well, to be fair, *she* had argued about how James usually got everything he wanted so he had no right to complain about not getting the last helping of dessert on this one occasion. James refused to argue back, in that smug, superior way of his, and went out to play football in the park with his friends. Grace stomped around the house, pretending not to sulk but actually being in the worst mood possible. A sudden urge gripped her to read *The Horse and His Boy* by C. S. Lewis, a book of hers she had lent to James two days ago. Retrieving it would involve going in James's bedroom (from which she was banned) and rummaging through his stuff. Well, it wasn't her fault if he was a slow reader, was it? It was her book and she wanted it back, simple as that. She rootled about in his room for a bit, enjoying the feeling of invading his private space, until she spotted the book on a high shelf next to the window. Hurriedly, she dragged James's long black sports bag towards her and stepped on to it, stretching up to reach the shelf ...

CRUNCH! TWANG!

She realised her mistake instantly. It hadn't been James's sports bag she'd stepped on. It had been the soft leather case he kept his guitar in. Heartbeat racing, she unzipped it. The mess of tangled strings and splintered wood she had found inside made her feel sick. James had had this guitar since he was seven. It was called a Gretsch Falcon. Shiny, white and beautiful, it had belonged to their late uncle Simon, who had toured the world in a jazz band. James practised constantly, doting on the instrument like it was a beloved pet. He beamed with pride whenever he played it with the school band. He was going to play it at their grandma's birthday party in a couple of weeks, as he did every year, to the delight of the whole family. *Classical Gas.* Well, not this year, he wasn't. Grace had felt a sudden burst of rage. *Idiot! Why did he leave his stupid guitar lying around on the floor if it was so flipping precious?* This feeling had been swiftly replaced by one of the darkest and doomiest dread. Her face and arms had begun to prickle unbearably. It had been an accident, of course. But she knew there was no way on Earth she'd be able to prove her innocence. Her brother, her parents, the whole family – everyone was going to despise her.

And there was more. Grace was already on her second warning from their parents about breaking James's stuff. On Christmas Day she'd trodden on one of the controllers of his new game console, snapping its joystick, after James had giggled when she'd sat on a mince pie in her best dress. And only last week Mum and Dad had given her a serious talking-to for playing roughly with a pottery penguin James had made in Art (she'd snapped its beak off). One more strike and they had promised her 'big, big trouble'. They hadn't specified what that meant – which was kind of scarier to Grace than if they had, leaving her to muse on what kinds of horrible punishments they might invent to inflict on her. Sometimes she thought no punishment could be as bad as the look of simple disappointment on Mum's and Dad's faces. Just thinking about it made her writhe with shame.

With terrible certainty, Grace had realised there was no coming back from the guitar incident, even if she let James have all the bread and butter pudding in the world. The shame would be everlasting. Panic coursed through her veins. She'd shoved the guitar case far under James's bed and had gone straight to her room for the rest of the evening, trying desperately to blot the possible consequences from her mind. Any distraction – even strange visitors babbling about far-off wars – was extremely welcome. And who knew? Maybe this girl really was offering her a chance to escape the shame and punishment that was heading her way? Saving the world might even prove a good way to make up for her blunders.

Grace picked up the sword.

2

Wellingtonia

A short while later, Grace stood outside the front door of her house, dressed in Grace-of-the-Field-of-the-Bubbling-Brook's armour and her second-best pair of trainers (she had a suspicion this Worthy War business might involve mud). From her waist dangled the sword Swickstipe in a walnut-coloured scabbard. In one hand she held the scowling bronze helmet. Over her shoulders she had slung her favourite backpack, which was shaped like a cartoon frog, and which contained her phone, the remainder of her week's pocket money (£1.02), three-quarters of a bar of boring plain chocolate that had come with one of her Easter eggs and on which she'd been nibbling aimlessly for over a month, a small bottle of mineral water, a bar of soap, a notebook and her special four-colour biro. Grace couldn't think of any situation she might encounter that would require her to be able to write in four different colours, but it was an epic bit of stationery and having it to hand made her feel good.

What lay ahead was unknown but that had to be better than definitely getting in the worst trouble of her life.

Right?

'Wellingtonia, the Sacred Steed, will explain what happens next,' Grace-of-the-Field-of-the-Bubbling-Brook had told her. And as she'd mentioned, she'd been more than willing to assume Grace's life until she got back from Brokenshire (ending the Worthy War would take a few days, tops, she'd promised), even if it meant taking the rap for James's busted guitar. Her plan was simply to lie in Grace's bed until she died, which seemed a little melodramatic to Grace. She didn't even seem that ill, really. In fact, she'd asked for some toast and something to read before Grace went off to battle. Dying or not, Mum and Dad might go easier on her for the guitar business if they could see she was poorly.

It felt absurd to be standing outside her house a little after midnight wearing a suit of armour. She tried to concentrate on the positives in her situation. A bunch of people wanted her to be their saviour, didn't they? Not James. Not anyone else in the world. *Her. Grace Parker*. Was she up for this challenge, whatever it might entail? *Yeah, too right, mate*. She'd show people she wasn't just the clumsy sister of Mr Perfect James Parker.

She *had* this.

She took a confident stride forward, misjudged the weight of her armour, overbalanced and fell into a flower bed.

As swiftly as she could, Grace hauled herself to her feet, trying to style out the fall as some kind of exercise. With some wariness, she approached the enormous white horse, which was still quietly cropping the front hedge. Dad was going to freak tomorrow when he saw the damage.

'Um, Wellingtonia?' began Grace. She had never talked to a horse before and it was hard to avoid the feeling that she was the victim of some elaborate prank. 'Hi? I'm Grace – the, er, *new* Grace.'

The horse swung its huge head towards Grace and regarded her squarely with two large brown eyes.

'So, you're number fifteen, are you?'

The horse talked!

Yeah, no biggie, thought Grace. *Just a talking horse.* She felt her legs turn to wet spaghetti. 'Er, yeah,' she replied in a half-stunned monotone. 'Grace Parker of 18 Marigold Avenue, Flakebury, reporting for duty.' She smiled as nonchalantly as she could, as if holding conversations with horses was something she did every day, and not a terrifying ordeal that made you want to run back inside your house, bolt the door and hide in a cupboard.

'You look weak. How many people have you killed?'

'Killed? I haven't killed any people. I'm only twelve.'

Wellingtonia snorted loudly. 'And how many slate dragons have you slain?'

'None. We don't get them around here so it's not really a skill you need to learn.'

The horse rolled her big brown eyes. 'And I daresay you'll tell me you haven't assassinated any venom goblins, either?'

Grace shook her head. 'Nope. Sorry.'

Wellingtonia gave a contemptuous whinny. 'And you are meant to be our saviour! You are supposed to lead the People of the Day to victory in the Worthy War! To vanquish the Fearsome Foe! The Fifteenth Grace! You, who have killed nothing!'

'Oh, I've killed lots of things,' said Grace. 'I once wiped out twenty-five neon tetra in a single day.'

Wellingtonia's small sharp ears pricked up. 'Oh, well, that sounds more promising. What are neon tetra?'

'Very small fish,' said Grace. 'I accidentally unplugged the aquarium heater in my school and they all died of cold overnight. To be honest, they're not really terribly robust creatures. In fact, it's quite hard *not* to kill them.'

Wellingtonia heaved a sigh. 'What hope is there

for the world when its champion is so wretched? We may as well give up and surrender to the People of the Night now.'

'Hey, hold your horses. Oh, sorry. No offence. What I mean is, I'm the Fifteenth Grace according to the prophecy thing the other Grace told me about, right? Like it or not, saving the world is down to me. So let's get on with it, eh?' Once more, the suspicion occurred to her that none of this talking horse and ancient prophecy stuff was really real, that she had somehow found herself caught up in some complicated game. Still, it was an excellent distraction from the dreadful trouble she knew she'd be in as soon as the guitar blunder was discovered.

'I suppose we must at least try,' said Wellingtonia. She knelt down on her forelegs. 'Climb aboard, then.'

Grace attempted to clamber into the horse's saddle, but the heavy armour restricted her movements and she kept losing her footing and sliding off Wellingtonia's flank.

'What are you doing?' demanded Wellingtonia. 'Come on. Stop wasting time.'

'Er, sorry,' said Grace. 'It's just that I've never – y'know – *got* on to a horse before and I'm not a hundred per cent sure what it is exactly you have to—'

Wellingtonia rolled her large brown eyes. 'Put down the helmet first. You can tie it to that strap hanging from my saddle if you like. Then grab the reins, put your left foot in the stirrup and swing your other leg over.'

'Gotcha. Hey! I did it!'

'About time,' said Wellingtonia and stood up.

Grace's stomach lurched. 'Whoa. It's really far off the ground up here.'

'Let us not delay further,' said Wellingtonia. 'The Army of the People of the Day is amassed outside Crumblechester and in need of a Grace's inspiration. The Fearsome Foe will soon show their accursed face.' Wellingtonia clopped out of the front garden and set off down Marigold Avenue at a steady canter. The street was dark and deserted.

'I thought you said the place we're going was called Brokenshire?'

'Crumblechester is the capital of Brokenshire,'

said Wellingtonia with thinly disguised impatience. 'Must our saviour be ignorant as well as weak?'

'This is my first day as a saviour actually so cut me some slack, eh?'

They continued along Marigold Avenue in moody silence. It was a still, star-flecked night and the *click-clack* of Wellingtonia's heavy hoofs resounded off the darkened houses. Grace wondered what the neighbours might think if someone looked out of their window now and saw her riding down the middle of the street on horseback. Then she realised she didn't care. If it meant avoiding the fallout for breaking James's stupid guitar she would have happily cartwheeled down the road barefoot across cat sick and broken glass.

'How do we get to this Brokenshire place anyway?' asked Grace. 'I've never heard of it before.'

'The very same way Grace-of-the-Field-of-the-Bubbling-Brook and I arrived. Through a rip in the very fabric of space.'

'You serious?'

'As death itself. Why do you ask?'

'That's the kind of stuff you get in stories.'

'This is no story!' snorted Wellingtonia. 'This happens to be true!"

'If you say so. Where is this rip thing?'

'Here,' announced Wellingtonia as she turned into the driveway of a house near the end of the street, 'in the garden shed of 44 Marigold Avenue.'

'But this is Mrs Winterbottom's house!' said Grace with an incredulous laugh. 'She's a dinner lady at my school! Are you really saying Mrs Winterbottom is a secret agent for some strange army fighting a bizarre war?'

'Not really,' said Wellingtonia. 'She just lets us borrow her shed occasionally. Nice woman.'

With a mighty hoof, Wellingtonia pushed open the flimsy gate standing at the side of the house. 'Your coming was foretold so it was considered convenient to locate a secret entrance to Broken-shire close to your family home.'

In the middle of the back lawn of 44 Marigold Avenue, Grace saw a perfectly ordinary garden shed made of thin planks of varnished wood and with a roof of rough grey felt. Her uncle Gareth had one like it in his own garden that he used for restoring vintage motorbikes. In front of the shed was a small ornamental pond encircled by a ring of large, roundish whitewashed stones.

Grace clambered down from the saddle. 'So, this is how you arrived in our world? Through this shed?'

Wellingtonia nodded. 'Yes. Although, strictly speaking, you and I inhabit the same *world*. It's just that the county of Brokenshire is separated from the rest of England – what we call the Mainland – in its own little pocket of space, like a sort of invisible floating island. There is a long and fascinating history behind Brokenshire and this is not the time to go into it.'

'Cool,' said Grace, striding towards the shed and edging her way carefully around the pond. 'I'm quite into long and fascinating histories. I read every one of the *Mr Men* books when I was little.'

'Come back!' hissed Wellingtonia. 'At once!'

'Huh?'

'Come back! Quietly and gently! Try not to tread so heavily!'

'Why?' asked Grace. 'What's the problem? It's

30

not like I'm going to fall in.'

There was a sudden rush of bubbles from the pond and the long, pointed snout of an enormous white shark burst from the water, its cavernous mouth open wide to display rows of jagged dagger-like teeth. The shark lunged towards Grace, who squealed and leaped backwards violently with a sudden strength born of terror. The shark snapped its jaws mere centimetres from Grace's face with a sound like the slamming of a dungeon door before sliding back into the pond and vanishing beneath the water.

Grace collapsed panting on to the lawn beside Wellingtonia. 'OK,' she spluttered, 'I have some questions.'

'I expect you do, impetuous fool,' said Wellingtonia. 'Go on, then. Ask me.'

'All right. Why is there a massive shark in this pond? How does a massive shark even fit in a pond? How did you get past the massive shark when you arrived? And how do we get past it now?'

Wellingtonia nodded slowly at each question. 'To answer your enquiries in order: It's a guard

preventing unauthorised access to and from Brokenshire. It fits in the pond because the pond is somewhat deeper than it appears. Grace-of-the-Field-of-the-Bubbling-Brook and I were able to get past it when we arrived because it was expecting us. We will be able to get past it now because I shall introduce you.'

'But it tried to bite my face off,' said Grace. 'I'm not sure I want to be introduced to anything that's tried to bite my face off.'

'Oh, don't be so wet and come and meet the shark,' said Wellingtonia sharply. 'She's called Alice.' She trotted up to the pond and stuck her head under the water.

'Be careful!' hissed Grace. 'She looked hungry.'

A steady stream of small bubbles issued from the pond. After

a moment, Wellingtonia withdrew her head and shook it to remove the water from her coat. A moment later, the shark's long white snout poked out of the water again and grinned a terrifying dagger-toothed grin at Grace. Grace eyed the enormous fish suspiciously. Then she noticed there was something stuck to one of its huge teeth: a reddish-brown lump of rubbery meat.

'All good!' cried Wellingtonia. 'Alice says sorry for trying to attack you but wants you to know that she was only her doing her job and you're not to take it personally.'

'No worries,' said Grace. 'Does Alice know she has something stuck in her teeth?'

'That's for you,' said Wellingtonia. 'It's a little present from Alice to apologise for trying to bite you. Please take it.'

'A present?'

'Yes, go on. And be quick about it.'

Smiling politely to disguise her fear, Grace reached out and pulled the lump of meat from the shark's tooth. It was cold and slimy.

'What is this?'

'A piece of seal liver,' said Wellingtonia. 'A shark's favourite food. Quite the delicacy. You should be honoured she wants to share it with you. Few humans ever get to taste it.'

Keen to create a better impression and make up for her previous display of fear, Grace raised the lump of slimy meat to her mouth. Just the smell was enough to make her stomach churn. *Come on*, she told herself. *You can do it.* She took a deep breath and went for it. It was like biting down on a slab of raw jelly that had been used to clean out a particularly filthy aquarium. Chewing slowly, she tried not to let the disgust register on her face, wincing uncontrollably as the cold, bitter meat slithered down her throat. Undeterred, she took another bite. Then another. In time she had finished the entire ghastly lump. As she swallowed the final repulsive mouthful, a foul-smelling burp erupted from her stomach and she felt a wave of nausea pass through her entire body. Blinking, she steadied herself against Wellingtonia, determined not to be sick or embarrass herself in any way, and gave the shark a cheery thumbs-up sign.

'Err, yeah. Delish. Thanks. Happy days.'

'Most impressive!' exclaimed Wellingtonia. 'I was going to say we should fry the seal liver with some butter, garlic and mushrooms and serve it up with some chips to make it more pleasing to the human palate. But you clearly couldn't wait, could you?'

'Wait, what?'

With a friendly wink, Alice the shark retreated to the depths of the pond, the water frothing in her wake.

'Now then,' said Wellingtonia, 'before we journey through the rip, there are a few facts you should know. You see this saddlebag hanging against my right flank? Unbuckle it and remove what you find in there.'

Grace obeyed and took out from the saddlebag a thick book bound in ancient-looking, cracked, grey leather. Its cover showed the profile of a man with a long white beard and was inscribed with a large teardrop shape.

'What's this?'

'*The Holy History of Brokenshire*. The works of

Soros the Sacred Song Singer. Trace your finger across the teardrop shape.'

'What?'

Wellingtonia snorted irritably. 'Do as I say, child. Swipe your finger across the cover.'

Grace did so, her finger sliding over the teardrop-shaped indentation in the old leather. As far as she could tell, nothing happened.

'What am I supposed to be seeing?'

'Is it not working? Try again.'

'I'm trying,' said Grace, running her finger over the leather binding once more, 'but I don't think it's doing any good.'

'Blast it,' said Wellingtonia. 'There must be no signal in this part of the world.'

'You mean like Wi-Fi?'

'I mean,' said Wellingtonia, 'like magic. This is a magic book and if we were surrounded by the magical air of Brokenshire all sorts of enchanted visions and songs with useful information would be erupting from its pages.'

'Sounds like Wi-FI to me,' said Grace. 'What happened? Did you forget to pay the phone bill?'

'No matter,' said Wellingtonia. 'We'll do it the old-fashioned way. Turn to page 114. And be quick before someone sees us.'

Grace thumbed through the book, its thick parchment pages crackling like damp logs on a fire, until she found page 114. It showed a complicated diagram something like a family tree with lots of little portraits of people and animals interconnected by criss-crossing lines.

'What's this? Medieval Facebook?'

'This,' said Wellingtonia, 'is a chart illustrating the two clans vying to rule the county of Brokenshire: the People of the Day and the People of the Night. Both control roughly equal numbers of towns in the county. You should attend it well and learn the names of those fighting the Worthy War. On one side we have the People of the Day. We run the county at the moment. People like Sarah Fairchild, Lord Clearwing, Captain Siskin and so on. At the top there you can see our leader, Mary Mugwort.'

Grace giggled. 'She looks like a frog.'

'Yes,' agreed Wellingtonia. 'That's because she's a toad.'

'And it says these guys on the other side of the page are the People of the Night,' said Grace, examining the diagram. 'Rowan Snipwell, Cardinal Axminster, Marwood the Storm-Robin … it says their leader is called Scarlett Moss.' Grace squinted at the illustration. 'Is she a bat?'

'A bat, yes,' said Wellingtonia. She flicked her huge head at the page. 'And look here, at this column beside the People of the Day.'

'The Saving Graces,' read Grace, 'and all the pictures look like me. What's that about? The other Grace looked like me, too.'

'Was there a lightning strike on the day you were born?'

'A lightning strike?' Grace stared in wonder at Wellingtonia. 'Yes! Mum and Dad told us that there was a big storm while Mum was in hospital giving birth to us. The lightning struck one of the buildings and set it on fire.'

'That lightning came from Brokenshire. Soros tells us the very landmass itself created its own saviours, stamping its mark on the girls who would deliver it from its enemies. You Graces are the children of the county of Brokenshire.'

'So these other Graces are like my sisters?'

'In a sense.'

Grace examined the pictures. It was crazy to think she had a whole string of relatives she knew nothing about. 'There's Grace-of-the-Laughing-Meadow, Grace-of-the-Jackdaw's-Wood, Grace-of-the-Dew-of-the-Blossom-of-the-Sweet-Hills ...'

'She was a good one,' interjected Wellingtonia. 'Enormous hands. Could take out a venom goblin with a single punch.'

Grace traced the line of names. 'And it goes all the way up to Grace-of-the-Field-of-the-Bubbling-Brook and then ... Grace Parker of 18 Marigold Avenue, Flakebury.' The illustration above her name showed Grace in her school uniform. 'Wow. How cool!'

'The Graces are fifteen young women bound by a sacred, unbreakable prophecy to lead the Army of the People of the Day,' said Wellingtonia. 'When one is injured or dies, the next takes her place. This is how it happens and how it *must* happen. You are the

Fifteenth and Final Grace. If the prophecies come to pass, as they must, you are the one who will save us. I'll admit I'm not terribly confident about your ability to do so. You seem about the weakest, slowest-witted and least prepared Grace I have ever encountered. But who am I to argue with the divine wisdom of Soros the Sacred Song Singer? Perhaps you possess some kind of hidden power or talent?'

Grace wrinkled her nose. 'Not massively, to be fair. But I'm up for anything that gets me out of having to face the music – or lack of it, ha ha – back home. I broke my brother's guitar, you see.'

Wellingtonia snorted. 'Ridiculous, clumsy child.'

'Hey, there's a picture of you here, Wellingtonia,' said Grace, pointing at one of the illustrations. 'Wellingtonia Jones,' she read, 'Sacred Steed of the Saving Graces, thirteenth daughter of Apollonia Jones, Empress of Shimmering Steppes …'

'I really hate that picture,' said Wellingtonia. 'It makes my ears look all flat.'

'There's a wiggly line coming from under your name,' said Grace. She followed it across the page with her finger.

'Pay it no heed,' said Wellingtonia. 'Put the book away. Time to go.'

Grace gave a little gasp. 'It leads to the People of the Night! To a horse called Olive Willow. It says she's something called the Flower of Death, Wielder of Soulscraper, Scourge of the Innocent, Most Wicked and Cruel Commander of Scarlett Moss's Personal Guard. Ooh, that doesn't sound nice. Do you know her, then?'

'We're *acquainted*, yes,' said Wellingtonia sharply. 'Distantly, I might add. But never mind that now. It's time we were elsewhere.'

She tapped the door of the shed with a hoof. Obediently, it swung open. Stooping, she stepped inside, her hoofs clattering loudly on the wooden floor.

'Follow me and close the door behind you.'

Grace obeyed. The interior of the shed seemed perfectly normal. There were a couple of bikes leaning against one wall and a rough wooden bench covered in dusty plant pots. A few old hammers and saws hung from nails.

'So, this rip-in-space thing,' said Grace. 'How

does that work? Is it going to be some crazy tunnel with weird patterns and you and I fall down it screaming with arms and legs flailing everywhere? Because I'm not sure my stomach could take it after that seal liver.'

'That all sounds most undignified,' said Wellingtonia, turning her huge body awkwardly in the cramped space to face the door, 'and it is not how rips in space operate. We have in fact already arrived at our destination. The very act of closing the shed door is sufficient to trigger the transition from the Mainland to Brokenshire. Open it and see for yourself.'

3

Welcome to Brokenshire

Grace yanked open the shed door and stepped outside. The first thing she noticed was an acrid stink that spiked her nostrils. She covered her nose and mouth with her hand. The second thing she noticed was the blackness everywhere. It wasn't the comforting, enveloping blackness of night she had just left. It was the blackness of things destroyed by fire.

She stepped outside on to a carpet of soft grey ash streaked with soot. She opened her mouth to say something but it was as if the words were frightened to come out. Her lips felt dry as dust. Her mind reeled at the abruptness of the transition from her own street, with its comfortingly dull rows of houses and parked cars, to this scene of desolation.

We've actually travelled … ! But this place … something terrible has happened here.

Charred ruins lay in every direction. The scorched remains of strange towers, cabins, huts and other buildings. She saw a large circular structure ringed with carvings in the shape of miniature boats, each one twisted and fire-blackened. Nearby teetered a vast wheel made of wooden struts as high as a church spire, now no more than a crumbling skeleton.

'Was this … a fairground?'

Wellingtonia stepped from the shed. She nodded. 'Rocky Stark's Far-Out Fun Plaza. It used to be my favourite place in the whole of Brokenshire. My daughter and I would come here every summer when she was little. She used to love riding the River Carousel. This was before I was called to be the Sacred Steed of the Saving Graces.'

Grace stared at the devastation. 'What caused this?'

'The Army of the People of the Night did this. All it took was a single blood-blaster to cause all this damage. Thank goodness it was out of season and there was nobody here.'

'Blood-blaster?'

'Blood-blasters, the fiery folk, exploding gnomes – they have many names. They're a race of tiny people who can blow themselves up at will. They re-form instantly without harm to themselves but cause absolute devastation to the surrounding area if the blast is powerful enough. Something to do with blood chemistry, I believe. And magic, of course.'

Grace's eyes widened. 'You have real gnomes here?'

'We have all sorts of things you don't have on the Mainland,' said Wellingtonia. 'The *Holy History* will tell you more. You can read on the way. Come on – time to get back in the saddle.'

Grace put her foot in the stirrup and climbed on to Wellingtonia's back. This time she managed it with ease. This felt like progress of a sort. If clumsy Grace Parker could learn how to mount a horse, maybe she could learn how to save the world, too.

'Where are we going?'

'Severton, an outlying district of Crumble-chester. A few miles from here. It's where the main fighting is currently taking place. Mary Mugwort is leading our army until you arrive.'

'And what exactly am I supposed to do when I get there?' asked Grace.

'Take command. Inspire your soldiers. Face the Fearsome Foe and vanquish them.'

Grace's nose wrinkled. 'Who is this Fearsome Foe? And how fearsome are we talking? Slightly fearsome and quite easy to beat? Because I think I'd prefer that to mega-fearsome and totally impossible to beat.'

'No one knows,' said Wellingtonia. 'The prophecies do not give the identity of the Fearsome Foe, merely stating that they are the People of the Night's champion and the most awesome warrior in all their number.'

'Hey, what was that?' said Grace suddenly.

'What?'

'Didn't you see it? It was something moving. Over there by the wheel.'

Wellingtonia was silent for a moment as she looked in the direction Grace was pointing. Her large nostrils flared, sampling the acrid air. The ruined fairground was as still as a tomb. 'I think we need to get going as soon as possible,' she said. 'Hold on tight to my reins.'

A deafening crash broke the silence. Grace watched in horror as the ragged remains of the fairground's huge wheel began to collapse, sending out clouds of soot and ash that billowed towards them at tremendous speed. The ground shook and now more of the fire-damaged structures began to fall in on themselves, unbalanced by the tremors.

Wellingtonia let out a whinny and galloped away in a bid to outpace the ash cloud. Grace clung to the reins, her knuckles turning white as she bounced painfully up and down in the saddle. She craned her neck to risk a look backwards and saw the black billow racing towards them like an angry wraith. Her heart somersaulted.

After a minute of furious galloping, the cloud behind them began to thin out and before long it had dispersed completely into the air. As they reached a patch of scrubby grassland bordered by hedgerows, Wellingtonia slowed to a halt and turned around. Barely anything remained of the fairground except for the shed and a few defiant struts of charred wood poking from a vast sooty stain on the landscape.

'Something did this,' said Grace. 'Pushed over the wheel, I mean. Some kind of creature. I couldn't see what it was.'

'That means there are enemy forces in the area,' said Wellingtonia gravely. 'We must stay alert.' She set off at a brisk trot.

The sheer cruelty and pointlessness of destroying a fairground gnawed at Grace's heart. 'Why would the People of the Night want to do this, anyway?' she asked. 'What's in it for them?'

Wellingtonia gave an exasperated snort. 'Evil people do evil things. That's about all one can say. What I do know is, they must be stopped – and soon – before it's the end of us all. And this is where *you* are needed.'

Grace felt her initial bluster harden into resolve.

There was definitely a battle to be fought here. A worthwhile one. And they clearly needed a leader. But should it *really* be her? That remained to be seen.

'I'll do what I can, Wellingtonia.'

As they made their way through the threadbare countryside, Grace tried to wrap her head around the fact that she was in a place no one had ever seen before. Or at least, that no *Mainlander* had ever seen before. What had Wellingtonia said about the county of Brokenshire being some kind of island? She scanned the landscape ahead and suddenly felt a peculiar fluttery feeling in the stomach, as if she'd just stepped off a roller coaster.

'Wellingtonia?'

'Yes?'

'Where's the sky?'

'The sky, you say?'

'Yeah, the sky. There isn't any. When you look into the distance, there's no horizon. The ground seems to curve upwards.'

'Ah, yes,' said Wellingtonia. 'It does that here.'

Grace tried to remember what she had learned

about 3-D shapes in Maths. 'Are we on the *inside* of something, then? Like the inside of a sphere?'

'More or less,' said Wellingtonia. 'Most authorities agree that the county of Brokenshire is more teardrop-shaped than actually spherical. It's all explained in the *Holy History*. Take a look. The book should work properly now.'

Grasping Wellingtonia's reins in one hand, Grace reached down and carefully removed the ancient book from the saddlebag. Experimenting, she ran her finger along the teardrop symbol inscribed on the cracked leather of its cover. Instantly, the world melted away and she found herself floating in a featureless white void. In panic, she paddled her arms and legs but found she was as stuck as a butterfly pinned to a collector's board. Then, some way off in the distance, she noticed a string of enormous letters apparently carved out of rock floating serenely in space. They spelled out the words:

The Holy History of Brokenshire

and then beneath in smaller letters:

Being the true and inerrant words of Soros the Sacred Song Singer. A Dart-Hagger publication.

Grace blinked. Now she was on Wellingtonia's back again, riding through the fields, a thin breeze tousling her hair. She noticed she had taken her finger off the book's cover. She replaced it on the teardrop symbol.

Now she was back in the white void, the words once more hanging impossibly in the air in front of her.

Another blink and she returned to Wellingtonia's back.

'I get it now,' she said, pleased with her own deduction. 'It's like virtual reality, isn't it?'

'I wouldn't know about that,' said Wellingtonia. 'What I do know is the book is magical. Now we're in Brokenshire, its magical abilities have been reactivated.'

'You mean we're in Wi-Fi range now? Cool.'

'You can scroll through the contents page or you can simply ask the book questions aloud and it will answer.'

'Like a smart speaker, then?'

'Is that some kind of Mainland wise person?'

'It's not a person. It's this round thing Mum and Dad bought. It sits on the coffee table and answers your questions.'

Wellingtonia frowned. 'Are you sure you don't have magic on the Mainland? Anyway, you'll probably want to turn off all the book's singing. It can get quite wearisome after a while.'

Grace ran her finger along the indentation in the book cover. Instantly, she zapped back into the white void. The huge stone words loomed in the distance.

'What's up with the shape of Brokenshire?' she said aloud in the slightly formal voice she always used when addressing her family's smart speaker.

There was a pause – and then a large stone question mark appeared in the air in front of her. She waited to see what would happen next. Nothing did. She scratched her chin, contemplating popping out of the void to ask Wellingtonia what the problem was, but then she decided to press on, determined to work things out herself. The floating question mark reminded her of error messages you got when you typed the wrong thing into a computer. What had she done wrong? She'd simply asked a question. Maybe you had to phrase things in a posher way – computers (and this book was feeling increasingly to Grace like a kind of computer) sometimes got confused when you used slangy language. She cleared her throat.

'Why is Brokenshire shaped like … whatever it is shaped like?'

Her phrasing wasn't very elegant but at least the question had been in straightforward English. She waited.

The question mark vanished. Music started to play. It sounded like some old-fashioned stringed instrument. A harp? Or what were those little guitar things? A lute? Yes, it sounded like a lute.

'*In days gone by,*' sang a voice. It was male and rather nasal-sounding.

'*Our fair county was wedded to the ground,*'

But nowadays, it floats on high from gravity unbound …'

Grace wrinkled her nose. Not exactly chart material. She remembered what Wellingtonia had said about turning off the singing.

'Turn off singing,' she said hopefully.

The song stopped abruptly. Now a fresh string of stone words appeared floating in the air.

Concerning the shape of the county of Brokenshire.

A series of images appeared. They were in high-contrast black and white, and reminded Grace of old-fashioned woodcut

illustrations her Art teacher had once shown the class. These depicted what looked like a meteor hurtling through space and slamming into the ground, sending up fragments of rock and other debris. The nasal voice began to narrate:

'Concerning the shape of the county of Brokenshire. Many years ago, Brokenshire was part of the Mainland. But one fateful day a huge meteor struck the Earth. Usually, this would simply create a large hole in the ground known as a crater, but on this occasion something very unusual happened. A recent earthquake had loosened the bedrock on which Brokenshire sat, so when the meteor slammed into ground nearby, the entire county got flipped into the air like a pancake, folding in on itself and forming the familiar inside-out teardrop shape that Brokenshire has today. This all happened so fast, and with such tremendous energy, that the loose county got shunted into its own little pocket of space and to this day hovers invisible and untouchable over the Mainland.'

An image appeared showing what looked like a vast teardrop made of grey rock. Labels appeared identifying places on the inside of its surface: *Crumblechester, Smashscape, Crackley.* The pointed end of the teardrop was identified as *Dart-Hagger Tunnel* (*No unauthorised access due to dangerous twisting in space-time*).

'*Over the centuries that followed, life on the Mainland took its own course. Most of the animals living there forgot how to talk. Many, like dinosaurs, venom goblins and lightning slugs, died out completely and now exist only in Brokenshire. The first humans to discover the county were witches and wizards escaping from persecution on the Mainland, their brooms and other forms of magical transport able to penetrate the secret pocket of space that surrounds Brokenshire. Their descendants now form Brokenshire's human population. These days, travel between Brokenshire and the Mainland is mostly facilitated by the creation of space-time rips …*'

Grace felt herself buffeted. She blinked and found that Wellingtonia had come to a halt in front of a large, rough-edged square hole in the ground. It was dark and looked very deep.

'What's the matter? We can go around it, can't we? Don't tell me there's another shark down there we have to be nice to.'

'It's not that,' said Wellingtonia. 'Look at those

grooves in the earth around the hole. There are fragments of what looks like armour around it, too. There's been some kind of struggle here.' She trotted over to the edge of the hole. Both she and Grace peered down into its depths but all they could make out was a gloomy blackness. Wellingtonia backed up a few paces and swung her large head back and forth, scanning the surroundings, her small ears twitching attentively.

'Hello … ?' called a voice from the depths of the hole. It was faint, with a lingering echo, as if it had been carried on the wind from many miles away. 'Is there someone there? Hello?'

Grace gave a small gasp. 'There's someone *down* there!'

4

Jonathan

'Hello? Please help! I'm starving to death down here!'

'Hello!' called Grace. 'Don't worry! We'll get you out!'

She slid *The Holy History of Brokenshire* into her backpack, dismounted from Wellingtonia and raced to the edge of the hole. It looked terribly deep. She tried not to think about the awful injuries a person might sustain if they fell into it.

Wellingtonia took the end of Grace's hair in her teeth and yanked her backwards.

'Ow! What are you doing?'

'A moment, child,' hissed Wellingtonia.

'What?'

'In case you failed to notice, we are at war.'

'Yes? And?'

'And,' said Wellingtonia with the air of a peeved headmistress, 'we don't know who's down there. It could be a friend. Or it could not. If they're one of the Army of the People of the Night then down a deep, dark hole is probably the best place for them.'

'I thought I was supposed to be the saviour,' said Grace. 'What's the point of being a saviour if you can't save anybody?'

'What's the point of saving someone who might go on to kill hundreds of your friends?'

'Maybe they'll be so grateful for being saved they won't?'

Wellingtonia snorted and shook her head. 'I don't think you realise quite how evil the People of the Night are. They're monsters who despise everything about us People of the Day. They spend their time plotting about how they can hurt us, kill us, wreck our lives. They won't be happy until they've destroyed everything we care about.'

'But we don't even know if the person down there *is* one of the People of the Night, do we?' said Grace.

'I'm not!' called a faint voice from the hole. 'I'm one of the People of the Day, like you!'

'Stay out of this!' shouted Wellingtonia into the hole.

'But there must be some way we can tell,' said Grace. 'Isn't there some code word or something that our side would know but the other side wouldn't? Please?'

Wellingtonia narrowed her eyes, thinking. 'Hmm. There's no code word that I know of but there is something I think only a Person of the Day might know …'

'What is it?'

'Hush, child.' She lowered her head to the hole. 'Hello down there. Can you hear me?'

'I can hear you!' returned the voice faintly.

'Very well. Answer me this. And if you get it wrong we shall tip a bucket of hungry leeches down the hole.'

'Bit harsh,' said Grace.

Wellingtonia shushed her.

'I understand,' came the voice from the hole. 'Go on.'

'Tell me,' called Wellingtonia, 'what is the first line of the *Prayer for the Morning of Salvation*? The prayer taught to every Person of the Day in their first year of school.'

'Easy!' called the voice. 'It's *Blessed by far are the Daylight Folk while those of the Dark should rot.*'

'Is that right?' asked Grace.

'It is,' said Wellingtonia. 'It's unlikely a Person of the Night would know that.' She called into the hole. 'Your answer is correct. What's your name, friend?'

'Jonathan,' called the voice. 'I am Jonathan Vetchling of the Vetchling Clan of Eagle Rock.'

'And what happened to you?' asked Wellingtonia.

'I was travelling to Shardley Market three days ago when I stumbled into this trap. I clung to the side and nearly got out but two of the Army of the People of the Night attacked me and I fell to the bottom. I've been slowly starving ever since. Who are you?'

'Wellingtonia the Sacred Steed and the Final Grace.'

'The saviour herself and her holy mount! I am honoured!'

Grace felt an unexpected flush of pride. *The saviour, eh? That's me.* She hoped she would prove worthy of the title.

Wellingtonia directed Grace to take a rope from one of her saddlebags, tie one end to her saddle and throw the other end into the hole.

'Ready?'

'Ready.'

Wellingtonia took the strain on the rope and took a step forward. Her muscles tensed. 'My word,' she muttered through gritted teeth. 'If this is what he weighs when he's starving I dread to think what he weighs with a full belly.' With slow, agonised paces, she hauled steadily on the rope, inching away from the hole. The veins in her neck and flank bulged out like snakes.

'Let me help,' said Grace and took a firm hold of the rope. She tugged at it hard, to no apparent effect.

'Let go, idiot child,' gasped Wellingtonia. 'If the rope breaks, it'll cut your hands to shreds, gauntlets or no gauntlets.'

Grace let go of the rope and raised her hands aloft moodily. 'Fine,' she muttered. 'Nobody needs stupid, clumsy Grace Parker's help, eh?'

'I'm nearly there,' called Jonathan. 'Just a few more feet …'

A large grey shape was emerging from the hole. It was roughly the size of a small car and covered with roundish scale-like tiles made of some hard, shiny material. Then Grace noticed a pair of tiny nostrils and under two bony ridges, a pair of small yellow eyes …

She backed away, her stomach seeming to fill with ice water. The creature's shape was familiar to her from countless films and television programmes – and more than a few nightmares. Her foot skidded on a rock and she fell heavily backwards on to her bottom, eyes still fixed on the huge, scaly animal. She opened her mouth to scream but all that came out was a feeble croak.

'So kind, so kind,' Jonathan was saying as his vast

grey body rose into view. He clutched the rope in a ridiculously small two-clawed arm. His other arm, Grace noticed, was missing. Shaking her head to clear it, she clambered to her feet and sprinted over to Wellingtonia.

'Stop! Stop pulling! It's a T. rex!'

Wellingtonia squinted at her through eyes half-closed with the effort of pulling. 'What did you say?'

'It's a T. rex,' said Grace. 'A dinosaur! It'll eat us!' She started to untie the rope from Wellingtonia's saddle.

'Leave it! Fool!' barked Wellingtonia. 'I'm pulling him out.'

'But it must be one of those People of the Night. Dinosaurs of the Night. Whatever.'

'We've already established he's on our side. Now run along and help him. Take him some food and water from my saddlebag.'

'But you said the other side are monsters!'

'Monsters, yes. Not dinosaurs.'

Grace opened her mouth and then closed it again. She felt her face start to flush.

'Go and help him. And then you can apologise afterwards for your disgraceful manners.'

'I ... OK.'

'Nearly out,' called Jonathan cheerfully. 'Just a few more feet should do it.'

Grace had the distinct impression he had been politely ignoring their conversation. She looked in Wellingtonia's saddlebag and found a metal flask of water and some small cakes. Hardly a feast for a hungry T. rex. Hang on. T. rexes were carnivorous, weren't they ... ?

With a final grunt, Jonathan hauled his huge body over the edge of the hole and collapsed panting on the ground. His vast scaly belly rose and fell like the inflating and deflating of an enormous balloon.

'Goodness me,' he wheezed. 'I thought I'd end my days in that horrid pit.' With another grunt he rolled on to his side and used his enormous sea serpent of a tail to lever himself into a standing position. Upright, he was a breathtaking sight, as tall and sturdy as an oak. He yawned. Inside the pink cavern of his mouth, his long teeth gleamed like rows of knives.

Grace approached him, heart thudding. She found she had to consciously persuade her feet to take each step. She held out the metal flask and a handful of the small cakes. Her hands were trembling, making the cakes on her palm wobble.

'Um, there's some food and water if you want it. It's not much. Still, better for you than a tiny girl in armour and a stringy old horse, eh?'

Jonathan lowered the gigantic bulk of his head down to Grace's level and sniffed at the offerings.

'These cakes,' he said. 'Are they vegan?'

Grace gave a splutter. 'Vegan? Are you saying you're a *vegan* T. rex?'

Jonathan nodded. 'Yes, well, I don't mean to make a fuss, obviously. Don't think I'm not grateful or anything …'

'They're fine,' said Wellingtonia. 'They're made with wintergreen milk.'

'Splendid,' said Jonathan and with tremendous delicacy lifted the cakes from Grace's hand with his fearsome teeth.

Grace winced, feeling the dinosaur's hot, sticky breath on her hand. She had a vision of the creature suddenly emitting a terrifying snarl and biting her in two. She tried to put it out of her mind.

Jonathan threw back his head and swallowed the cakes in a single gulp. Then he used his one tiny arm to take the metal flask and emptied its contents into the fleshy cave of his mouth. His long pointed tongue swished back and forth.

'Thank you,' he said, returning the flask to Grace. 'It's my absolute honour to be saved by the Final Grace herself.'

Grace stared in bewilderment. 'I've just met a T. rex,' she muttered. 'That's wild. And it can talk. That's even wilder. But a T. rex that's a vegan? That's some other, new level of wild.'

Jonathan regarded her with his tiny yellow eyes. 'Is it any wilder than eating the flesh of another living creature?'

'I wish we had time to indulge in philosophical debates,' said Wellingtonia sternly, 'but we need to get this young lady to the front line of the fighting where she's needed.'

Jonathan rose to his feet with a springing motion that actually made the ground vibrate a little. 'Of course. And I'll accompany you. You saved my life so the least I can do is make sure you get there safely.'

'Your offer is appreciated,' said Wellingtonia, 'but there is really no need.'

'If he wants to help, shouldn't we let him?' said Grace. 'Having a gigantic dinosaur on our side can't be a bad thing, can it?'

'There's no mention of a dinosaur assisting the Final Grace in the Sacred Songs,' said Wellingtonia uncertainly. 'I don't like going against them. It might upset the entire prophecy.'

'But I bet they don't say there are definitely *no* dinosaurs involved either.'

'That's true,' Wellingtonia conceded. She gave a loud snort. 'Fine. Join us, then, Jonathan.'

'It's my privilege to assist the Final Grace,' said Jonathan in a reverent voice. 'I'll do everything I can to help. I'm handy in a tight corner, I promise.'

Grace beamed. The big dinosaur's simple enthusiasm gave her a feeling of encouragement.

Wellingtonia motioned to them both with her head. 'Come, child. Jonathan. Time to go.'

'Which way now?'

'To Severton. Via the Crystal Chasm.'

'That sounds cool,' said Grace.

'It's actually incredibly dangerous. The chances we might perish are high.'

'I'm happy to take a less cool route if it means we won't die,' said Grace.

'I wish we had that option,' said Wellingtonia.

5

A Discovery

For some time the three of them travelled across the sparse, scrubby countryside of Brokenshire. It was difficult for Grace to tell exactly how long had elapsed because there was no sun visible. Instead of a blue sky overhead there was just a pale grey-brown fuzz – the far-off opposite side of this bizarre, inside-out county.

'What happens here when night falls?' asked Grace.

'It gets dark,' said Wellingtonia.

'*Ha ha*,' said Grace flatly. 'How can it when there's no sun?'

'What's this "sun"?' asked Jonathan.

'A big fiery ball, so I've read,' said Wellingtonia. 'It's where our daylight and heat come from. The world flies around it once a year. Apparently you can actually see it from the Mainland.'

'Is that true?'

'Oh yeah,' said Grace.

'Can you see it from your hometown?' asked Jonathan.

'Now and again when it stops raining.'

'Gosh! The Mainland sounds like an amazing place.'

'Definitely doesn't feel like that when you're there.'

A wooden sign ahead announced they were entering the village of Crushing.

'Not too far to go now,' said Wellingtonia. 'After Crushing it's the Crystal Chasm and then Severton lies beyond that.'

Crushing was almost as dilapidated as the fairground. Houses lay in ruins. Stone cottages smoked gently under the scorched remains of thatched roofs. The abandoned debris of everyday life – books, bits of furniture, stray items of clothing – littered the streets in gloomy little piles like drifts of snow. A grim silence hung over everything. Grace shivered. She could almost feel the sadness in the air. 'Where is everyone?'

'Went south to avoid the fighting, I imagine,' said Wellingtonia. 'The prophecies speak of most battles being fought in the north. There must be hundreds of families wandering displaced.'

'All this stuff just left behind,' said Grace, looking around. 'It's heartbreaking.' She tried to imagine her own family uprooted from everyday life – Mum, Dad, James and her forced to flee their home, not knowing if they'd ever return. The idea made her queasy. Grace noticed a teddy bear lying in the gutter. She clambered down from Wellingtonia's back and picked it up. It looked a sweet little thing. Gently, she stroked its fur.

The teddy bear opened its jaws. 'Gerroff me, you dippy wench!' it snarled and bit her wrist. Grace screamed and dropped the creature, which made a rude gesture and then scuttled off into some bushes.

'It was alive!' she whined, rubbing her wrist. Fortunately, its teeth had not pierced her skin.

'You have bears on the Mainland, don't you?' asked Wellingtonia.

'Yes, but – well. Never mind.'

Jonathan was pawing through the torn remains of a large book with his single hand. He emitted a sad little grunt.

'What's up?' Grace asked.

'Haven't seen this in years. It's a recipe book. We used to have it in our cave at Eagle Rock. I learned how to bake scones from it when I was little. My first vegan recipe. Shame half the pages have been torn out.'

'I'll have a look for them,' said Grace. 'They might be lying around somewhere.' She scanned the piles of debris scattering the ground. 'Aha!' She scooped up a couple of pages that looked like they came from a cookbook. There were more lying in crumpled piles dotted here and there. Methodically, Grace collected each one, smoothing out the creases and assembling them in page order. 'By the way,' she said, grunting as she reached under a rickety three-legged table to retrieve another handful of pages, 'if you don't mind me asking, what happened to your other arm? Did another dinosaur bite it off?'

'No,' said Jonathan. 'I was born like this.'

'Oh blimey,' said Grace. 'Sorry. I hope I haven't offended you.'

She straightened up quickly and found herself face to face with a gigantic brown bear. Her stomach lurched. The bear stood well over seven feet tall on its hind legs and was glaring at her with two tiny black-brown eyes. Around its belly and legs were faint stripes of shaggy white fur matted with dried mud.

Remembering her manners and not wanting to repeat the embarrassment with the shark and Jonathan, Grace held out her hand politely. 'Hi. I'm –'

The bear snarled thunderously. It swiped at her with an enormous claw, catching her with a rough pad across the side of the face. It was like being hit with a shovel. Grace screamed and felt herself plough into the ground, all air smashed from her lungs. Disorientated, face numb, she raised her head and saw the bear slam a foot on to her back, pinning her to the ground.

'Guys ...' she croaked, holding a hand out towards Jonathan and Wellingtonia, who were hurrying towards her.

'Release her, you filthy beast,' bellowed Wellingtonia, her long face setting into an expression of grim determination. She curled her lip and put her head down, preparing to charge.

'Whoa there, 'orsey,' called an amused voice. It came from overhead. Grace and Wellingtonia looked up to see a much smaller bear – in fact, Grace recognised it as the one which had bitten her earlier – perching on top of Jonathan's head, a tiny sword in its paw. The tip was touching the top of Jonathan's skull. 'Now, don't do nuffink clever like trying to rush me,' said the bear, 'or dino-boy 'ere gets my blade through 'is brain. OK?'

Jonathan gritted his enormous teeth.

Wellingtonia snorted furiously but remained where she was. Grace blinked, dazed. The small bear grinned. Its teeth were tiny and very sharp.

'That's 'ow we like it, innit? All nice and friendly.

77

And what a class of friend it is! Going up in the world, I am. In every sense. Stone me if it ain't the Final Grace 'erself and her equine pal the Sacred Steed. I recognised your mugs from the *'oly 'istory*.'

'I got her, Chris,' hollered the big bear in a loud, dull voice. 'I got her. Look!' He patted Grace with his enormous claw, making her groan.

'Yeah, I know that, Ron,' said the small bear. 'You big dozy sack of manure. I 'ave eyes, you know, and I'm perfectly capable of seeing for myself that you 'ave the Final Grace under that dirty great foot of yours.' He poked the top of Jonathan's head a few times with his sword. 'Take me over to Ron. And no funny business or I'll spike your noggin and use it for a conker. OK?'

'Whatever you say,' said Jonathan in a quavering voice and ambled over towards the big bear that had Grace pinioned to the ground with its foot. The enormous T. rex looked absurd to Grace with the tiny bear sitting on the top of its head.

'Lean down a bit,' commanded the small bear.

Huge nostrils flaring with indignation, Jonathan lowered his head until the small bear was at eye level with the big bear. The small bear beckoned the big bear forward with his claw. The big bear leaned towards the small bear, curious. The small bear took his sword and struck the big bear squarely on the nose with the hilt. The big bear jerked back his head with a loud grunt, apparently more surprised than hurt.

'There you go, Ron,' said the small bear with a laugh. He resumed sticking the end of the sword against Jonathan's skull. 'Stupid lump. Think twice before interrupting me again now, won't ya?'

'Yes, Chris. S-sorry, Chris,' said the big bear quietly.

'Dunno why I put up with 'im, I really don't,' said the small bear. 'Like dragging around a great rock all day, it is. Being lumbered with him. 'Cept I'd prob'ly get more sense out of a rock. See those white stripes 'e 'as? That's 'cause he's part polar bear. Notoriously lazy, your polar bear. Notoriously thick, too. Not like us browns.'

'Sorry, Chris,' repeated the big bear.

'Shut it,' snapped the small bear. 'Now where was I? Oh yeah! Only about to become the grand 'ero of the People of the Night, wasn't I? Single-'andedly capturing the Final Grace and her Sacred Steed! My word! We all knew the Prophecies of Pertle the Pious Poet was gonna come true, but I never guessed I'd 'ave such a pivotal role in the final battle myself! Why, Scarlett Moss 'erself will probably knight me once I present her with you two. And your pet newt here.' He laughed and stamped a tiny foot against Jonathan's head. The T. rex gave a wince of terror.

So these are People of the Night? thought Grace. They were as horrible as Wellingtonia had told her. She guessed this Pertle the Pious Poet must be their version of Soros the Sacred Song Singer. But if Pertle's prophecies were different to those of Soros, which were actually true?

'Oi, 'orsey!' called Chris. 'You got your nosebag with you?'

Wellingtonia glared at him. 'What of it?'

'Where is it?'

'Folded up in my saddlebag with my other—'

'Fine,' snapped the little bear, cutting her off. He nodded at Grace. 'You. Get up off the floor and get your 'orse's nosebag. No funny stuff or this sword plunges straight into this scaly monster's brainbox.'

Dizzy and aching, Grace crawled out from under the big bear's gigantic foot and opened Wellingtonia's saddlebag. From inside she removed a plain grey feedbag with a long strap for tying around a horse's head.

'Tie it on 'er,' said the small bear. 'But tie it over 'er eyes, so she can't see.'

'Over her eyes?'

'Stone me, you're as bad as Ron! Do you want me to come down there and give you some of what I gave 'im?'

'No,' said Grace quickly. She and Wellingtonia exchanged a look of patient understanding before Grace began to tie the feedbag around the horse's eyes. 'Sorry about this,' she muttered as she pulled the straps into a tight bow.

'Bide your time,' said Wellingtonia quietly. 'The moment for action will come.'

'All right, no chit-chat,' said the small bear. 'We all nicely blindfolded there?'

'Yes,' said Grace.

'Luvverly. Now, 'ere's 'ow it's gonna work. I'm taking you lot with me as prisoners to our glorious leader Scarlett Moss. Me and the dinosaur will go first. The girl will lead the horse and Ron will bring up the rear and tear any of you to pieces if you attempt any of the aforementioned funny business. Clear, m'dears?'

'And then we'll see the trigger wolf?' said the big bear. 'I wanna see the trigger wolf!'

'Shut up! Shut up!' hissed the small bear, making a slicing gesture at his neck with his free hand. 'Oh, nice one, you big dummy. Tell the 'ole world, why doncha?'

Wellingtonia let out a pained whinny.

'What's a trigger wolf?' asked Grace.

'None of your flipping business, young lady,' said the small bear. 'That's what it is. And don't you forget. Right, I've 'ad enough of 'anging around 'ere with you tomfools. Walk on!' He stamped his tiny foot against Jonathan's head. 'You 'eard me! Walk!'

*　　*　　*

The sad little procession trudged out of Crushing. Chris, the small bear, chattered constantly from his perch atop Jonathan's skull – mostly about how clever and brave he was to capture three members of the People of the Day, including the Final Grace herself, about how richly the leader of the People of the Night, Scarlett Moss, was going to reward him and about how he would get even with everyone who had ever crossed him in the past. Behind them, Grace led the blindfolded Wellingtonia by her reins, the big horse stomping her hoofs and exhaling furious blasts of hot air from her nostrils with every step. At the back marched Ron, the big bear, his small eyes and long snout devoid of expression.

Occasionally, when Chris's ranting was at its loudest, Grace and Wellingtonia found they could exchange brief snatches of whispered conversation.

'Where are we now?' hissed Wellingtonia, during one of Chris's monologues. 'What can you see?'

'We're walking beside a river,' replied Grace.

'Wait. It's not a river of water. It's a river of rock. Shiny transparent rock. Dips down in a massive V shape. Looks nice. Shame we can't take a moment to appreciate the scenery.'

'That's the Crystal Chasm,' said Wellingtonia. 'It's the way we were headed. Where the river cuts through a huge plain of rock crystal. The sides are so slippery that if you fall into it you can never climb out. Hundreds have lost their lives there over the years.'

'In that case, I'll move us away from the edge.'

'We're near the edge?'

'Slightly. A bit. We're fine now. Honest.'

'Foolish child.'

After a while they arrived at a narrow stream of water that snaked across the landscape and emptied into the gleaming depths of the Crystal Chasm.

'Can we stop here, please?' croaked Jonathan. 'I need a drink. My throat's as dry as a cream cracker.'

'No, we can't, you lazy lizard,' snapped Chris. He prodded Jonathan's head with his sword. 'Keep going!'

'But if I collapse of thirst,' said Jonathan, 'I might fall on you and squash you like a grape.'

'Change of plan!' announced Chris to the party. 'Five-minute rest break. You may drink at the stream. My, what a generous master I am to you lowlifes.'

Gratefully, Jonathan lowered his head to the stream and began to lap at the cool water with his thick, snake-like tongue.

With a look of childish glee, Ron lumbered to the edge of the stream and dipped his huge clawed feet in the water. Instantly, a mud-coloured cloud appeared around each foot. The big bear sighed with pleasure and flexed his clawed toes.

Chris gave a bitter laugh. 'Look at 'im. Great filthy brute. He'll pollute the 'ole of Brokenshire with the muck clinging to 'im. That's the polar bear blood in 'im, see? All that snow and ice destroys the brains. Thick as treacle, the lot of 'em.'

Grace couldn't help smiling at the sight of Ron enjoying the water. The big bear suddenly seemed more like a frisky puppy. She took the bar of soap from her backpack and offered it to him. Ron put his snout next to it and sniffed.

'No, thank you. I already ate.'

'It's not food,' said Grace. 'It's soap. You clean yourself with it. Like this.' She mimed using the soap to wash.

'Oh. OK.'

Using the tips of two long claws, Ron took the bar of soap from her delicately. He wet it in the stream and rubbed it against his belly as Grace had demonstrated. A thick white lather began to form. He rubbed again, rinsing the area with a clawful of stream water, and patches of brilliant white fur began to emerge.

'My stripes!' he gasped. 'My polar bear stripes!'

'They look cool,' said Grace.

'They *are* cool,' agreed Ron. 'Very, very cool, in fact. They ain't looked this cool in years.' He stared at her, as if seeing her for the first time. 'Thank you, girly.'

'You're welcome.'

Wellingtonia cleared her throat pointedly. Grace gave her nose a quick pat. 'I think we *might* have a chance to get out of this,' she whispered to her. 'Cross your hoofs.'

Ron resumed washing himself with renewed vigour, stopping every so often to rinse away the foaming lather. Within the space of a minute, he had removed every inch of dirt from his fur, which Grace now saw was a beautiful glossy nut brown, his lower abdomen and back legs streaked with bands of perfect white.

'Turns out there was a rather handsome bear under all that dirt,' said Grace with a smile. 'Who knew?'

Ron plunged his head into the stream and pulled it out. He spat a joyful arc of water into the air. 'There was. I feel great!'

'Well,' said a voice, 'you *look* ridiculous.'

Chris was perched on Jonathan's head, arms folded, his tiny snout curling in a sneer. 'I dunno why we don't just tie a pink ribbon around your head and use you as a prize on a coconut shy. You're supposed to be a war bear, you enormous idiot! Dearie me. I curse the day we was brung together as a team. They only done it 'cause we're both bears. I told 'em I 'ad nothing in common with no halfwit polar bear half-breed but they wouldn't listen. It's a miracle I've achieved what I 'ave, 'aving to put up with your gross thickheadedness. I preferred it when you was caked in mud. Least then I didn't notice all those stupid white stripes …'

A loud sob erupted from Ron's long snout and the big bear dashed off towards a clump of trees. As he sped away, his huge feet pounding on the ground, Grace could hear that he was crying. She turned to Chris.

'You've upset him now.'

'Good!' cried Chris. 'He deserves every word of it, the work-shy clod. Have no fear, he'll be back when his little tantrum's over. Knows what side 'is bread's buttered, that one.'

'Maybe he won't be back,' said Grace. 'Maybe you've pushed him too far this time?'

'I doubt it,' said Chris – but then a look of uncertainty crossed his face. He shook his head, dispelling the thought. 'Nah. 'E'll be back, I'm sure of it.'

'What if he isn't?'

Chris flexed his claws nervously. Then he gave a sly smile. 'Maybe he won't come back. And maybe that's no bad thing. Plans can change easy enough, can't they? Who needs prisoners anyway? Pain in the neck taking you lot all the way to Mary, ain't it? Maybe I should just kill the three of you right now? Starting with this T. rex.' He gripped his sword tightly in both hands, as if preparing to drive it deep into Jonathan's skull. Jonathan let out a shriek and shut his eyes tightly.

'Please,' implored Grace, a wave of panic rising inside her. 'There must be another way.'

'There is another way,' said Chris. 'And this is it! You gave me this idea, wench! This is all your doing!' He laughed uproariously and raised his sword high.

There came a thumping sound. The ground trembled very slightly.

Chris and Grace looked around to see Ron bounding towards them on all fours. His eyes were blazing with fury. Droplets of stream water were flying from his fur.

'*My. Stripes. Look. Fantastic,*' he growled. 'Girly thinks so. And so do I.'

Chris stared at him in confusion and disbelief. 'What's got into you? You ungovernable creature. Calm down this instant!'

But Ron kept racing towards them. He bounded up Jonathan's long tail like a person hurrying up a staircase, his small brown eyes fixed on the smaller bear.

Chris made a feeble attempt at a laugh. 'You don't want to take it to 'eart, the things I say, Ron lad. Can't a bear have a bit of banter with his cousin?' He glanced down at the ground, as if judging if he could make the jump.

Ron had reached Jonathan's head, the T. rex bearing the extra weight with ease. Without pausing, he swept up Chris in one of his huge front paws and bellowed directly into his face.

'*My. Stripes. Look. Fantastic.*'

'All right, all right,' said Chris. 'No need to make a big deal out of—'

Ron drew back one thick, muscular arm and then hurled Chris away with all his strength. Grace watched as the small bear sailed through the air in the direction of the Crystal Chasm. He bounced along its smooth, crystalline side several times and then began to slide downwards with increasing speed.

'Can't we discuss this like reasonable bears?' he called faintly.

A moment later, he had slid completely out of view.

'*My. Stripes. Look. Fantastic*,' Ron bellowed again, his head raised to the sky. He leaped down from Jonathan's skull, landing beside Grace.

'Thank you, girly.'

Before she could reply, Ron bounded off towards the trees once more, muttering and laughing to himself as he went.

Jonathan let out a tremendous sigh and collapsed on to the ground in an enormous belly flop.

For a moment, there was silence.

'What's going on?' demanded Wellingtonia. 'Can't one of you remove this thing from my eyes?'

Grace untied the feedbag from around Wellingtonia's head. Wellingtonia blinked several times and shook her head.

'What happened?'

'Ron turned on Chris,' said Grace. 'Seems you weren't the only one who was close to the edge.'

'We mustn't delay,' said Wellingtonia. Her large

brown eyes were wide with what looked like fear. 'We must get to the front. Warn Mary and the others about this fresh danger.'

'What fresh danger?' asked Grace.

'You hear the bears. They said the People of the Night have a trigger wolf.'

'And that's super bad, is it?'

Wellingtonia gave a snort of impatience. 'It's about the worst thing imaginable. A creature of awesome destructive power. This must be the Fearsome Foe you will face!'

6

Shell-Shocked

At Severton, on the outskirts of the city of Crumblechester, tall wooden buildings leaned at crazy angles against one another like fallen dominoes. Most were peppered with large blackened holes.

The narrow streets were deserted of humans and animals. A few posh-looking wooden carriages lay abandoned here and there. But despite its emptiness, the place lacked the deathly silence of Crushing. Instead, the air was filled with a constant rumble like distant thunder. It was punctuated by occasional crashes and what sounded like yelling voices.

'What's that noise?' Grace asked Wellingtonia.

'That, child,' answered the horse, 'is the sound of the Worthy War. We're very close to the battlefront.'

Grace shivered. She had never heard an actual *war* taking place before. It made her tummy feel cold.

'I wonder if they're reached the Governor's Palace yet,' said Jonathan.

'I doubt it,' said Wellingtonia. 'They sound too close to us for that.'

'What's this about the Governor's Palace?' asked Grace.

'The People of the Day are officially in charge of Brokenshire at the moment,' said Wellingtonia. 'The Governor's Palace is where Mary Mugwort and our other leaders run our government. But the People of the Night want to capture it and install Scarlett Moss as governor of the county. And it now seems they have a trigger wolf to stop you interfering with that plan.'

'So what the flippity *is* a trigger wolf?' asked Grace. 'I keep hearing the words but so far no one has—'

Jonathan suddenly raised his single hand. 'Get down! Quickly! Behind that carriage!'

He shoved Grace to the ground behind the battered remains of a wooden carriage while he and Wellingtonia sprinted to take cover behind a low brick wall.

'What's going on?' hissed Grace.

With his single short arm, Jonathan pointed a scaly finger upwards.

Grace craned her neck — and saw a row of black shapes sailing through the air in formation over-head. They were large grey-black birds with sinewy necks and huge diamond-shaped wings. In their webbed feet they clutched large yellow eggs.

'Bomber geese,' said Wellingtonia. 'They're heading this way. Make yourself as small as possible. Perhaps they haven't seen us.'

Grace squeezed her body into a tight little ball and screwed her eyes shut. Once again, she heard

the rumble and shouts of the far-off fighting. Weirdly, the sound reminded her of the time she had walked past Flakebury football stadium when there was a home game on.

CRASH! CRASH! CRASH!

The three deafeningly loud impacts made Grace squeak with alarm. She guessed the geese had started bombing. She hugged her knees tightly. The air filled with the stomach-churning smell of rotten eggs. Choking, she placed a gauntleted hand over her face to block out the stench. Now she heard a voice calling:

'Tortoise gunners – *FIRE!*'

Warily, she opened one eye and saw an extraordinary sight. Six giant tortoises – each the size of a small car – were marching briskly down the street. Strapped to their shells were what looked like miniature cannons. As one, they halted, lowering their back legs to aim at the formation of geese overhead, and pulled strings attached to the cannons on their backs.

There was a loud cracking sound. Fire and smoke erupted from the tortoises' cannons. This was followed by a tumult of furious honking overhead from the geese.

'Tortoise gunners!' yelled the tortoise at the front of the group. 'Retreat!'

Now the six tortoises waddled away with surprising speed, their clawed feet clicking rhythmically against the road. They turned a corner and were lost from sight.

Grace removed her hand from her face. Fortunately, the stench of rotten egg seemed to be dispersing. Jonathan and Wellingtonia appeared from behind the wall.

'We're obviously closer to the fighting than I thought,' said Wellingtonia, stretching her neck and back as if they were stiff from her having to crouch. 'We must be extra careful with all this heavy shelling going on. Come on. The entrance to Mary's secret bunker isn't far from here.' She trotted off, nostrils flaring at the remnants of the bad egg smell hanging in the air.

Grace clambered to her feet and followed, Jonathan at her side.

Bomber geese dropping rotten eggs, tortoise gunners

with cannons on their shells … If someone had told Grace a couple of days ago she would be witness to these things, she would have laughed herself silly. They sounded like characters from a video game she might play on her phone. Home, her brother and his broken guitar seemed very distant now.

In reality, though, her legs were trembling and her stomach felt the way it did after too much ice cream.

'What's this about a bunker?' she asked, putting on a brave voice.

'Mary Mugwort has a secret bunker not far from here. It's where she and the rest of the leaders of the People of the Day are hiding out to formulate their battle plans. She'll help you face the Fearsome Foe.'

'Watch out, chaps,' said Jonathan. He pointed to a big yellow object lying in their path.

They halted. Grace saw a large yellow egg standing upright a few feet ahead of them. It looked like one of the ones the bomber geese had dropped. It seemed to have fallen into a patch of soft mud and not broken apart. But – there was a nasty-looking black crack running down most of its length.

'We should be fine if we tiptoe around it,' said Wellingtonia. 'But take care. If we cause a tremor it could burst open. And at this range the awful stench could knock us out cold.'

'How does a horse tiptoe?' asked Grace.

Wellingtonia rolled her eyes. 'Just be careful, child. For all our sakes.'

But before they could take another step forward, two long brown ears appeared over the top of the egg. Grace blinked at them in confusion.

Now a tall brown hare (the owner of the ears) dressed in a long black overcoat stepped out from behind the egg. It stood on its hind legs, and in its front paws it carried two hefty-looking wooden pistols.

'Good afternoon, my fine friends,' it drawled, pointing the pistols in their direction. 'Germander Speedwell, highwayman hare at your service. You would do well to place all monies, jewellery, snuff-boxes and other valuable effects you may have about your persons on the ground before me with all speed. And no false moves or I shall be obliged to blow you into tiny, tiny pieces.'

'A highwayman!' spat Wellingtonia. 'Here we are risking our lives to end this brutal war and selfish rodents like you have nothing better to do than go around robbing decent people!'

Germander made a scoffing sound. 'What care I for your war? The People of the Day and the People of the Night are both equally irritating, if you ask me. The only cause truly worth fighting for is that of Germander Speedwell. So, your valuables, and quick about it, if you please.' With a loud click, he cocked both pistols.

Heart thumping, Grace removed Swickstipe from its scabbard. 'Here. This must be worth a bit of money.'

Germander Speedwell eyed the gleaming sword. 'Oh, yes,' he cooed. 'That shall do nicely. Drop it. And be gentle. I'm quite sure these musket balls could penetrate your armour with ease.'

Grace tossed the sword lightly towards the hare. It skittered along the ground until its point struck the base of the egg. There was a loud cracking noise and the egg began to vibrate.

Germander goggled at the egg in fear. 'What

have you done, fool?' he demanded. 'That blessed egg looks like it's about to ex—'

There was another loud cracking noise. The egg split apart and a viscous yellow gloop exploded outwards at tremendous speed. But then there was a strange flash of red light.

Grace covered her face, waiting for the horrible contents of the egg to hit her – but then was surprised when she felt nothing.

'How extraordinary!' she heard Jonathan say.

She peeped through her gauntleted fingers and saw that the egg had somehow frozen mid-explosion. Bits of broken eggshell and trails of gloopy yellow slime were radiating from its centre, hanging motionless in mid-air. Even Germander Speedwell himself was frozen in place in the act of shielding himself from the exploding egg, standing still as a sculpture.

'What's going on?'

'Hello, m'dearios,' said a friendly voice. 'I take it you're here to see Mary?'

'Sarah!' cried Wellingtonia.

Grace watched as a young girl of about her

age ran towards Wellingtonia and threw her arms around the horse's neck. She was dressed in shimmering black robes and her hair was an extraordinary fiery pink colour.

'This is Sarah Fairchild,' explained Wellingtonia to Grace. 'She's a sorceress. And a friend.'

'Was that … magic?' asked Grace, nodding at the impossibly frozen exploding egg.

'I call it a time-out,' said Sarah. 'Neat little spell, ain't it? The effects don't last long, though, so we'd better get moving. Should be OK to get your sword now, by the way.' She gestured for them to follow her.

'I'm Grace,' said Grace, retrieving Swickstipe and wiping its blade on a patch of grass. 'Number fifteen.'

'A pleasure, m'dear,' said Sarah. 'I know a certain toad who would like to meet you very much.'

7

Underground

Sarah led them to a narrow street lined with rows of deserted buildings until she came to a tiny bookshop. A cheerful sign swinging above its door identified it as

Parkinson's Premier Reading Matter

She took a small key from inside one of her boots, unlocked the door and held it open for the others.

'Inside, m'dearios.'

'Why here?' asked Grace, eyeing the rows of brightly coloured spines lining the walls.

'Perfect hiding place,' replied Sarah. 'People who like to fight generally shy away from books.'

She led them into a small back room that was empty save for a large and dusty old rug covering the floor. Sarah lifted up a corner of the rug, revealing an enormous trapdoor. Quickly, she rolled back the rug and heaved the trapdoor open. A steep set of wide stone steps led downwards into blackness.

'Down we go. I hope you like spiders.'

Grace peered nervously into the darkness. 'A lot down there, are there?'

'No,' said Sarah. 'Just one big one. But he's very sensitive.'

The sensitive spider, whose name was Kevin, and who was the size of a car tyre, greeted them with a shy wave with four of his eight legs as they arrived at the bottom of the steps.

'Hi, Kev,' said Sarah. They were standing at the mouth of a long passage lit with lanterns. 'It's Kevin's job to guard the entrance to Mary Mugwort's secret bunker.' She gestured to Grace.

'And this is the Fifteenth Grace. Our saviour.'

'Gosh,' said Kevin and averted his eight eyes, his bristly face turning a bright shade of pink. 'What an honour to meet you.'

Grace had to smile. She had never seen a spider blush before.

The passage branched in several directions. Sarah instructed Jonathan and Wellingtonia to take one branch, where she informed them they could rest and get something to eat. Grace she directed to another branch.

'Mary's office lies at the end of this passage,' she told Grace. 'I'm sure she'll be excited to meet you.'

'Speaking of food ...' said Grace. She pointed at her own stomach.

'Destiny first, snacks later,' said Sarah and grinned.

After a minute of two of trudging down the gloomy passage, Grace arrived at a smallish oak door. She rapped her knuckle against it, feeling slightly nervous, as if she had been sent to the head teacher's office.

'Come in,' said a voice from within.

Grace pushed open the door and found herself in a pleasant office with wood-panelled walls. Behind an expansive wooden desk was a swivel chair. On it sat a large toad on a plush red cushion. Its knobbly skin was a dull olive green, its eyes two great lime-green marbles. On its head, somewhat bizarrely, sat a tiny, twinkling tiara.

'Mary?'

Grace watched as the great green eyes swivelled to take her in.

'And who have we here? Wait! That face! It can only be …'

'I'm Grace. The fifteenth one.'

Mary shifted excitably on her cushion. 'Goodness me! So our great war has not much longer to run! And are you ready for what lies ahead, Fifteenth Grace? Are you ready to fight and defeat your Fearsome Foe and save us all?'

Grace shook her head. 'To be honest, nope. I *have* found out what this Fearsome Foe thing is, though. Something called a trigger wolf. Whatever that is.'

Mary Mugwort's eyes grew even bigger. 'Oh my! I think I need to call a meeting.'

The meeting took place in a spacious, high-ceilinged room filled with rows of simple wooden benches. Lantern light made shadows flicker across the walls. It reminded Grace of a sea cave she and her family had explored once while on holiday in Crete. She sat down on an unoccupied bench and surveyed the others present.

Several humans and animals of various species sat dotted around with serious expressions on their faces. Grace noticed a large hairy pig dressed in tweeds and what looked like a fox with a bandage over one eye. She also spotted Sarah Fairchild, who gave her a friendly wave. Jonathan and Wellingtonia – both now looking fed and well-rested – and a couple of other large animals, including a stag with an impressive set of antlers, remained at the back of the room near an ornate fireplace.

At the front of the room, Mary perched on her red cushion, which had now been placed on a simple wooden stool. Her marble-like lime-green

eyes ranged over the faces of those present and she nodded to herself, satisfied. Then she cleared her throat several times and the chatter in the room ceased.

'I call to order this meeting of the War Council of the People of the Day,' said Mary briskly. 'Thank you all for coming. I have momentous news to share, friends, so listen well.'

Everyone leaned forward in their seat. Breaths were held.

'The fighting at Severton and at other parts of Crumblechester has now ceased thanks to a brave last push by the tortoise gunners. The People of the Night are thought to be preparing for a single, final attack on Crumblechester using what Soros refers to in prophecy as the *Fearsome Foe*. We shall hear more of this plan soon. But first, let me say how honoured we are today to have with us Grace Parker of 18 Marigold Avenue, the Fifteenth and Final Grace,' said Mary.

All eyes turned to Grace. She raised a shy hand. 'Er, hey, guys.'

'We all know what this portends,' continued

Mary. 'Fourteen previous Graces have fought and fallen as prophecy demanded.'

There were a few sniffles of sadness around the room as this news sank in.

'So now,' continued Mary, 'the Fifteenth is here to defeat the Fearsome Foe in the final battle that will lead us to ultimate victory in the Worthy War.'

Now a rousing cheer echoed throughout the room. The hairy pig dressed in tweeds punched the air with its trotter and whispered, '*Yes!!!*'

'However,' Mary went on, 'this task will be anything but easy. Intelligence has reached us that suggests the Fearsome Foe possessed by the accursed People of the Night is … *a trigger wolf.*'

Now a volley of gasps and distressed muttering rose up. Mary raised a large, spindly-fingered hand for silence. The noise died down.

'Some of you may not be aware of these creatures,' said Mary, 'so I have arranged a demonstration. Lord Clearwing – would you be so kind?'

A boy of about ten stepped forward. He had long sandy-coloured hair and wore a beautifully tailored coat and shoes with shiny buckles. He was holding a copy of *The Holy History of Brokenshire*.

'Thank you, Mary,' he said in a clipped voice. He ran a finger over the teardrop-shaped indentation on the book's front cover.

Immediately, a glowing image appeared, floating above the book. It showed what looked like an ordinary wolf cub with fluffy grey fur and a slightly darker muzzle. Its large round eyes looked bright and full of fun. It did not seem remotely dangerous.

'An ordinary-looking wolf of the non-speaking kind one finds on the Mainland,' said Lord Clearwing. 'Or so you might think. And you would be wrong. For the *Holy History* tells us this is a rare magical creature known as a trigger wolf. They are believed by some to be the descendants of an ancient wolf god. Others believe they are born from the acorns of a vast and evil oak tree. Whatever their origin, their power is certain.'

He swiped his finger over another section of the book's cover. Now the image of the wolf cub grew in size. And as the animal grew larger its eyes grew narrower and meaner, and its limbs became more muscular. Its jaws lengthened and opened to reveal ferocious teeth. It had very quickly become an image of unspeakable fury. Seeing it, Grace felt her throat suddenly tighten and her mouth grow dry.

'Whenever a trigger wolf becomes enraged it grows rapidly in size to roughly the height of a bron-tosaurus. An untameable fury then grips the beast. It embarks on a savage rampage of destruction. But, and here's the peculiar thing ...' Lord Clearwing raised a finger for emphasis. '... when in this mental state, the creature is drawn towards artificial struc-tures. Trees, rocks, hills it all ignores. But buildings, bridges, towns, cities, these things it seeks out – *and destroys utterly*. It is thought their ordered straight lines somehow infuriate the animal's chaotic nature. You can see, therefore, why a trigger wolf makes a tricksy and ingenious choice of Fearsome Foe. It cannot be reasoned with. It is stronger than a hundred other creatures put together and its single thought when roused is destruction!'

A fearful murmur reverberated in the small room. Somewhere a quiet voice exclaimed, 'Oh my good gosh!'

Grace raised her hand tentatively.

'You have a question?' said Mary.

Grace nodded. 'But how can they control it? Surely this trigger wolf poses just as much of a threat to the People of the Night as it does to us?'

'Our spy Corporal Parsnip has some information regarding this matter. Corporal Parsnip, would you … ?'

In the audience, the fox with the bandaged eye now stood up. He cleared his throat and spoke in a drawling, educated voice. 'When I was behind enemy lines there were rumours someone high up in the People of the Night was learning an ancient magical craft called *gwildeena*. The word meant nothing to me. I couldn't find it in the *Holy History* or any other reference work. And then one day, I was helping an old sow look for berries. This pig was as ancient a creature as I've ever met. I mentioned the word in passing as she said her grandfather had practised it many decades ago to shake acorns from oak branches. The word means *storm-tamer*. It is the ability to subdue and control any powerful natural force. I believe an adept of

115

this craft could succeed in making a trigger wolf do their bidding.'

There was another ripple of uneasy murmuring.

'Do we know who this student of *gwildeena* is?' asked Sarah.

'Her name,' said Mary gravely, 'is Olive Willow.' She looked sympathetically at Wellingtonia. 'I'm sorry to tell you this.'

Wellingtonia's voice came from the back of the room. It was thick with emotion. 'Once more, Mary, I can only apologise sincerely for the foolish actions of my wayward foal.'

Foal? thought Grace. *So Olive Willow is Wellingtonia's daughter! No wonder she didn't want to talk about her.* She turned around in her seat and saw Wellingtonia standing with her head down, her large brown eyes glassy.

Mary nodded sympathetically. 'Olive Willow's actions are her own. Which brings me to the next part of what I have to tell you. Our plan.'

The boy Lord Clearwing traced a finger over the surface of his copy of *The Holy History of Brokenshire*. A map appeared, floating in the air. Several places were marked, including Crumblechester. One area showed a tiny blue dot next to a wide blue line.

'We know Olive Willow is stationed in this old castle on the banks of the Rat Tail River, just a few miles from the city,' said Mary. 'It makes sense to assume that this is where she is practising her craft on the trigger wolf. The castle offers the space and privacy for such experiments. It lies on a slight rise from which the only artificial structures visible, other than the castle itself, are those of Crumblechester. Hence a trigger wolf emerging from it would head straight here, intent on destruction. We have also observed that all roads leading to the castle are currently being guarded by unusually large numbers of the People of the Night's Bear Battalion.'

'It was a couple of bears who let slip to me about the trigger wolf,' said Grace. 'They must be from the same battalion.'

'That seems likely,' said Mary. 'The area surrounding the castle itself is guarded by the army's Elite Assassin Force. Therefore, the Fifteenth Grace must lead a small team to infiltrate this castle, capture and subdue the trigger wolf, depriving the People of the Night of their Fearsome Foe and thus fulfilling the final prophecy of Soros the Sacred Song Singer to end the Worthy War.'

'About this Soros guy,' said Grace, a thought that had nagged her for a while finally crystallizing. 'If his prophecies are so good, why do we even need to do anything?'

Mary fixed Grace with a piercing stare. 'Are you trying to be funny, young lady?'

Grace laughed nervously. 'No, but you see what I mean? If what he foretells in his songs is true, won't it happen anyway?'

'This is exactly what the Tenth Grace thought,' said Mary. 'Grace-of-the-Thicket-of-the-Bitter-Bark. She too believed the prophecies would just fulfil themselves. And so rather than taking up her rightful role in the Worthy War, she stayed at home all day playing with her spinning top and eating carrot cake. She was meant to be fighting in the Battle of the Screaming Gate.'

'And what happened?'

'The Battle of the Screaming Gate came to *her*.

Her entire village was destroyed by rampaging nettle geese and venom goblins. She found her courage at the last minute and took up Swickstipe, eventually helping our army to the narrowest of victories. But too late to save her own family. This is the lesson of the prophecies. Yes, some sequence of events resembling the prophecy will come true. No matter what. But *how*, and with what sorrowful consequences, is down ultimately to us. To *you*.'

Grace frowned, chewing her thumbnail. 'Right. So let me ask you – if I can steal this trigger wolf, the Fearsome Foe, from the People of the Night, and stop it destroying the city, that's the end of war? Right? That would fulfil the prophecy?'

Mary nodded gravely. 'It would. But there is no guarantee that you yourself would survive.'

Grace gave a tiny smile. 'Happy days.'

8

Petronilla Saxifrage

Rested and fed herself now, Grace waited at the foot of the steps leading up into Parkinson's Premier Reading Matter. Kevin the spider lurked shyly nearby, the arachnid equivalent of a sheepish grin on his face.

Choosing her team for the raid on the castle had been what James would have called a *no-brainer*: Wellingtonia, of course. Sarah for her magical ability, which they hoped might help in subduing the trigger wolf. And Jonathan for his tremendous strength and courage. The three of them were waiting for her upstairs in the bookshop, restless to begin their mission. Mary had asked Grace to meet her by the steps because she had some final bit of information to impart before she left.

Grace wondered idly what was happening back at home. Was Grace-of-the-Field-of-the-Bubbling-Brook currently receiving the mother of all tellings-off for breaking James's guitar? It had been fewer than twenty-four hours since her menacing, armoured figure had burst into Grace's bedroom and yet, to Grace, it seemed as distant and unreal as a half-remembered dream. Brokenshire was her reality now.

'Grace?'

Grace blinked – and found Mary Mugwort standing beside her. The toad's tiara sparkled dimly in the lantern light. 'Before you leave on your mission,' she said in a grave voice, 'I have a gift for you.'

'Oh,' said Grace, slightly taken aback. Mary didn't seem the present-giving type. 'Thanks. What is it?'

'A surprise.'

'Cool!' said Grace. 'I'm very into surprises.'

But then Kevin the spider pulled a sack over her head and everything went black.

Grace felt herself bundled away and dumped into some kind of metal container, possibly a wheelbarrow, which was then rolled away.

'Guys? What's going on?'

She clawed at the sack over her head but found it secured by a thick and impenetrable knot. The wheeled container went over a bump and she felt herself lurch violently, the sack muffling her panicked squeal. Desperately, she clung to the container's metal edge. She felt it tilt, as if she was being propelled up a slope. A breeze ruffled the sack over her head and she realised she was outside.

On the container trundled. After a time, the journey became smoother and she began to suspect she was being propelled over grass. But then the container juddered to a halt and she felt herself pitch forward on to the ground.

Half-stunned, she sat up, her fingers exploring her surroundings. She'd been right about the grass. Groaning with effort, she scrambled to her feet, and, hands outstretched, took a cautious step forward.

Her fingertips touched a rough stone surface. A wall maybe? It was low and narrow, its top curved into a semicircle. Did that mean … ?

She heard the swift swish of a sword blade through the air and the sack over her head suddenly split into two pieces and fell away. When her eyes accustomed to the bright light she found herself staring at a gravestone into which were etched the words:

HERE LIES
GRACE-OF-THE-SUNLIT-SLOPES-OF-THE-CANTAKEROUS-MOUNTAIN

THE SEVENTH SAVING GRACE OF BROKENSHIRE

DIED AGE 15 SAVING THE BOROUGH OF FLECKHAMPTON FROM A MONSTROUS COPPING

'What's a gopping?' wondered Grace quietly to herself.

'If I told you,' said a gruff voice, 'you'd throw up on the spot and probably faint and fall in it and neither of us has sufficient time or cleaning products for that nonsense. So pay attention, eh?'

Bewildered, Grace spun around and found herself face to face with a tall skinny bird with sparse grey plumage and an enormous hooked beak. On its head it wore a tall hat with a buckle and with the tip of one wing it clutched a long glittering sword. She also noticed that they were standing in what looked like a graveyard, with several worn and ancient headstones standing in neat rows.

'Who are you?'

'Ma name, lass,' replied the bird in a thick accent, 'is Petronilla Saxifrage of the Fifteenth Dodo Dynasty of Skarbrick Ridge. Chief Sword Instructor to the Army of the People of the Day.

HERE LIES

GRACE OF THE SUNLIT SLOPES OF THE CANTANKEROUS MOUNTAIN

THE SEVENTH SAVING GRACE OF BROKENSHIRE DIED AGE 13 SAVING THE BOROUGH OF FLECKHAMPTON

Mary thought ya could probably do with a lesson to brush up on your swordswomanship before you went off on ya mission. What with the future of all of us depending on it.'

'OK,' said Grace, 'but was it totally necessary to put a sack over my head and push me here in a wheelbarrow?'

HERE LIES
THOMAS TROUTSHOE
BELOVED HUSBAND OF
LORETTA DEVOTED
FATHER OF
REGINALD, ELIZA AND DIRK

'Are you feeling flustered, annoyed and confused, by any chance?' asked Petronilla. 'Are you sweaty and uncomfortable? Is your heart beating a million miles an hour?'

'Yup,' admitted Grace. 'Pretty much all that.'

'Then that's how you should practise fighting. Enemies rarely come at you when you're feeling your best.'

Grace had to admit there was a certain logic to what the bird had said. 'Did you say you were a dodo?'

'Aye. What did ya think I was? King o' the sparrows?'

'No, sorry,' said Grace. 'I thought dodos were extinct, that's all.'

'Maybes tha' sleepy bunch on the Mainland have died out,' said Petronilla, 'but not here. And maybes if them others were half as good as me at wieldin' a sword, they'd still be breathin' today, eh? Speakin' o' which, draw your weapon, my lass! Let's see what ya got.'

'Oh. Yeah. Right.' Grace fumbled with her scabbard and heaved out the sword Swickstipe. 'There. Bit slow, I suppose.'

'Bit slow!' bellowed Petronilla. 'If I were a venom goblin I'd have ripped your throat out with ma talons by now. You're an absolute lemon!'

'Hey, I can handle myself,' said Grace, bristling. 'A boy once pinched my ice cream when I was at the beach and I chased him for half a mile and eventually tripped him up and made him eat sand until he handed it back. OK, he was five and I was nine but I was really proud of the way I handled the situation.'

'Ya little softie,' spat Petronilla. 'Ah sense you've sailed through yer Mainland life without true hardships of any kind.'

'You say that, but I was really looking forward to that ice cream.'

The dodo snorted through her bulbous beak. 'That right? You're a disgrace. You know that? Look at the way ya hold Swickstipe. Yer arm all limp like yesterday's asparagus. 'Tis an insult to the sacred blade. It's like you've never even been in a sword fight afore now!'

'I haven't,' said Grace. 'Sword fights aren't a big thing on the Mainland any more.'

Petronilla cut in impatiently. 'Wait. Ya mean ye

127

never had a sword-fightin' lesson in yer whole life?'

Grace shook her head. 'Nope.'

'That's preposterous!' said Petronilla. 'Every creature in Brokenshire gets sword-fightin' lessons when it's a child. How am I supposed to teach ya the finer points of this great art when ya don't even know the basics?'

'Beats me,' admitted Grace.

'As will every opponent you'll ever face,' said Petronilla gloomily. She sat back heavily on her scrawny, feathered rump. 'By 'eck! What are we gonna do with ya, lass? Soros's prophecy says you'll lead us to victory in the Worthy War wieldin' Swickstipe. But in reality – first hint of trouble and you'll be sliced in half before you've even got your sword in ya hand.'

'I can't help that, can I?' said Grace, turning away with a hopeless sigh. 'I didn't write the stupid thing.' She reached out and gently touched the weathered surface of the gravestone. 'Did you teach this Grace sword fighting?'

'Grace-o'-the-Sunlit-Slopes-o'-the-Cantankerous-Mountain? Aye, I did. I taught most o' the Graces. We dodos live a long time, y'know.'

'What was she like?'

'Oh, a fine fighter!' said Petronilla, a glint in her eye. 'So precise with the sword. Could poke the pip out of a grape from thirty yards. Every Grace I taught had their own unique style. Grace-o'-the-Dew-of-the-Blossom-of-the-Sweet-Hills was a proper bruiser, y'know? Used the sword like an axe. Tremendous power. Grace-o'-the-Ivy-o'-the-Ruined-Abbey, on the other hand, she was a clever one, real tactician. Lotsa fancy footwork and cunning plans.'

Grace held Swickstipe aloft proudly. 'Then maybe I've got my own unique style too and I just need to find it?'

'Forgive me, lass, but ah don't think "complete rubbish" is an actual style.'

'I mean it,' said Grace. She pointed Swickstipe at Petronilla. 'Come on. Come at me!'

'Don' make me laugh,' squawked Petronilla. 'I'd split ya in two.'

Undeterred, Grace jabbed Swickstipe forward and knocked off Petronilla's tall hat.

'Hey! Watch what ya're doin'!'

'Maybe you should stop me?'

'Ah will!' said Petronilla, clambering to her spindly clawed feet. 'Ah'll teach ya a proper lesson if ya don' behave.'

'Come on then,' said Grace. 'Teach me a lesson.' She didn't have the faintest idea what she was doing but it had to be better than sitting around and moping. And maybe, she thought, in the process, she might actually stumble across her own unique style of wielding the sword.

If she actually had one, of course.

'Ah'll try not to hurt ya too badly,' said Petronilla, expertly twirling her own sword. 'Ah don' wanna get in trouble wi' Mary for cuttin' the saviour to shreds.'

Chuckling, she waddled towards Grace.

Grace's heart lurched. She scurried behind the gravestone, putting it between her and Petronilla. The dodo lunged forward, her blade slashing through the air, missing Grace's nose by milli-metres. Grace shrieked and backed away.

'Maybe ah'll lop off one o' ya ears,' sniggered Petronilla. 'Just enough damage to remind ya ah don't mess about when it comes to swordplay.

Would that suit ya? Or how about a few toes? Ya could wear 'em on a string around ya neck! How pretty ya would look!'

Her sword arm already aching, Grace ducked behind another gravestone. This one was covered with reddish lichen and its faint, eroded inscription read:

HERE LIES
THOMAS TROUTSHOE
BELOVED HUSBAND
OF LORETTA
DEVOTED FATHER OF
REGINALD, ELIZA AND DIRK

Troutshoe? Grace blinked at the inscription. Her own mum's maiden name had been Troutshoe. As surnames went, it was highly unusual. There were only a handful of families in the country who shared it. Did this mean, somewhere in the distant past, her mum's family had originated in Brokenshire? It might go some way to explaining why Grace now found herself mixed up in the affairs of this extraordinary county …

THUNKKK!

Petronilla's sword slammed down on to the grave-stone, jolting Grace out of her contemplations.

'Ah have ya now!' the skinny dodo cackled.

The only thing Grace could think to do was thwack down Swickstipe on to Petronilla's blade, hoping she might be able to damage it, perhaps even sever it completely.

CLANNNNNNNGGGGG!

OWWWWWWWWWWWWW!

When Grace opened her eyes she found Wellingtonia gently tapping her arm with her enormous hoof.

'Huh? Whuh? Whah?'

'Nice to have you back with us, child. It's time for us to set off to the castle.'

'What?'

She sat up. She was back in the bookshop with the other members of the party. Mary Mugwort was there too, regarding her with amusement. She reached for her scabbard and found Swickstipe inside it.

'What happened? I was fighting with Petronilla.'

'A funny thing,' said Mary. 'We found you both fast asleep on the ground in the graveyard. That must have been a most fatiguing lesson.'

'Fatiguing?' Grace shook her head to clear it. She had no memory of anything that had happened after – what? She remembered seeing Thomas Troutshoe's gravestone ...

Mary chuckled and patted Grace's shoulder with her long greeny-brown fingers. 'Typical Petronilla. I knew the old dodo would work you hard. Finally found your own fighting style with Swickstipe, have you?'

'Oh yes,' said Grace quickly, not wanting to appear unprepared in front of Mary. She was the saviour, after all, and it was important that every-one had confidence in her. 'Absolutely yes. Definitely.' She smiled broadly and played with the ends of her hair, which was something she always did when she lied.

9

Mrs Smew

For hours they rode towards the castle where the trigger wolf was being kept, Grace on Wellingtonia's back and Sarah on Jonathan's. Jonathan wore no saddle or harness but Sarah was able to lash herself securely to the T. rex using a scarf, while holding tight to the thick, knobbly scales that ran the length of his spine.

The landscape of Brokenshire unfurled beneath their feet. Sometimes they passed mountains and lakes of breathtaking beauty. Other times they found themselves traversing featureless scrub. They waded through murky, treacle-thick swamps and splashed through watery, fern-bristling bogs. Above them, the sky – or what passed for the sky in this strangely remote section of England – remained the same eerie grey-green.

Grace's encounter with Petronilla Saxifrage had shaken her confidence. What would be the consequences of her not mastering the use of her sword? And why had she and Petronilla blacked out like that? She remembered what Mary had said about the prophecy coming true for Grace-of-the-Thicket-of-the-Bitter-Bark whether she liked it or not. She might well be the Saviour of Brokenshire – but at what cost?

A sharp cry of pain interrupted her thoughts. She looked across to see Jonathan pitch forward on to the ground, one huge foot snarled in a tough tangle of tree roots. Fortunately, Sarah was thrown clear of the stricken T. rex, landing in a damp ditch at the side of the road, bruised, mud-spattered but thoroughly grateful, no doubt, not to have been crushed under the dinosaur's enormous bulk.

Jonathan wriggled painfully into a sitting position, bending nearly double to cradle one ankle in his tiny hand. He winced. 'I think it could be sprained.'

Wellingtonia cantered over. She looked him up and down appraisingly. 'Can you stand up?'

'I – I don't know.'

With much groaning and sighing, Jonathan clambered to an upright position, balancing on his tail and good leg. Gingerly, he placed the other foot on the ground.

'Aaghh!'

'I think that means he can't,' said Grace.

'Don't you have any spells that can heal Jonathan's injury, Sarah?' asked Wellingtonia.

'Sorry, m'dear,' replied Sarah. 'Don't know any spells for mending reptiles' hurts. I could fix his injury but he'd be walking around with a human foot for the rest of his life and I shouldn't think he'd want that. Probably wouldn't take his weight, anyway.'

'So what are we going to do?' asked Grace.

'Just put an arrow through my brain,' moaned Jonathan. 'Then leave me here to rot.'

'Don't be so dramatic,' said Grace, patting his scaly hide. She scanned the surrounding countryside. Some way off she spotted a roof and chimney visible above a hedgerow. 'Looks like a farmhouse over there to me. They might know how to treat animal wounds.' She dismounted from Wellingtonia.

'Why don't you let me take you?' asked Wellingtonia. 'I can have you there in half the time.'

'We don't want to spook whoever lives there,' said Grace. 'I'll appear less of a threat if I don't turn up on the back of a massive armoured horse.'

'Very well,' said Wellingtonia. 'But be quick.'

'Yes, please do,' said Jonathan. He winced again.

The front garden of the farmhouse was awash with dancing yellow flowers. Grace had to look twice to check they were not *actually* dancing, merely waving in the breeze – you could never be sure in Brokenshire – but they looked to her like ordinary daffodils. She guessed plants did not share the ability to talk that animals in this county enjoyed. After meeting Wellingtonia and Jonathan, she'd more or less assumed that all Brokenshire animals could talk. But, now she thought about it, did that apply to even the tiniest insects? What about bacteria and viruses? *Imagine being infected by a virus that talked to you as it tried to kill you. Yuck.*

A narrow gravel path led up to the front door. A sign on it read

Private residence of Mr & Mrs Smew

Grace rapped hard three times. The sound reverberated away to silence. Just as she was about to walk away, she heard the clank of a bolt and the door opened a crack.

'Yes … ?' came a quavering voice from the darkness within.

'Hi,' said Grace. 'Is that Mrs Smew? I'm wondering if you can help me.'

'Help?' said the voice with a note of unease. 'Help how? I can't do anything. My husband's away at market. What do you want from me?'

'Not much,' said Grace. She tried to keep her voice cheerful and friendly. 'It's my friend, you see. He's hurt his ankle. I was wondering if you might be able to treat it.'

The door opened further, revealing a short,

wizened woman clad in heavy tweed clothing. Her nose was long and thin. Behind her thick-lensed glasses, her tiny squinting eyes looked like two currants rattling in a jam jar.

'Friend, you say?' She looked around suspiciously. 'Where is this friend?'

'He's on the road on the other side of the field. He caught his foot in something and tripped. He's a T. rex so he came down pretty heavily …'

'A T. rex?' repeated the woman in alarm.

'A very friendly one,' said Grace. 'He doesn't even eat meat. Can you do anything for him?'

There was a long pause while the woman considered this, her face expressionless. 'I suppose so,' she said eventually. She opened the door fully. 'Come in.'

With slow, painful-jointed steps, the old woman led Grace to the farmhouse's kitchen. It was a large room, but with a rather stuffy, stale atmosphere. Its floor was stone and there were rows of shelves filled with jars, many of them furred with dust. At its centre stood a huge wooden table with places set for just two people. Grace got the impression there had once been many happy family gatherings around this table, but that they had happened many years ago. At the rear of the kitchen was a sturdy door with a big, frosted glass window through which pleasant green-tinged light streamed from the garden.

'I'll make up a poultice for your dinosaur friend,' said Mrs Smew, taking a mortar and pestle from a drawer. 'Hold it against the ankle and the swelling will go down in no time. You'll have to fetch the ingredients for me, though, love. My eyes aren't what they used to be and I can't read the labels.'

'Fine,' said Grace. 'What do you need?'

'Chargreen powder, robingrass, yellow prince-weed, sage and poppledock.'

Grace found jars containing each of the ingredients – various odd-looking dried leaves, brightly coloured powders and weird, knobbly-looking roots – and brought them to Mrs Smew, who mixed them with some water from a jug and began to grind them together into a pungent, grey-blue paste. The old woman's movements were extra-ordinarily slow. Grace had to fight the urge to ask her to hurry, reminding herself she was lucky that Mrs Smew was helping them at all.

'Is it just you and Mr Smew who live here?' she asked, hoping to pass the time while the old woman painstakingly crushed the herbs. She glanced around the kitchen. There was a definite air of sadness about the place.

'Oh yes,' she said, adding wistfully, 'it is *now*.'

'Did you have children?'

'Indeed we did, love. Six strapping young sons. All away now fighting the Worthy War. Just when we need them here.'

'For working on the farm, you mean?'

'That. And other things.'

Grace frowned. 'What do you mean?'

Mrs Smew shook her head. 'Oh, listen to me blathering on! You can't stand around all day listening to a silly old woman's woes. Let me get a jar for this poultice. Just apply it to the wound and wrap a bandage around it good and tight. It ought to work just fine on a dinosaur's hide.'

There came a loud rap at the back door. Through its frosted glass window Grace could make out the

silhouette of a person. They looked thin and extraordinarily tall.

'Shall I get that for you?'

Mrs Smew waved a hand. 'Don't bother yourself, love. I'll see to it in a moment.' She handed her a stoppered jar filled with the grey-blue poultice. 'Here you are.'

'Thanks.'

'Can you see yourself out? I've got to deal with the ... my *visitor*.'

'Sure,' said Grace. 'Thanks again.'

She placed the poultice jar in her backpack, zipped it up, waved to Mrs Smew and headed out of the kitchen. As she placed her hand on the handle of the farmhouse front door, she heard a bang and a scream. The noises had come from the kitchen. She turned back, a spark of strange fear igniting in her belly. She heard raised voices: Mrs Smew's high, warbling tones and another lower, thicker voice. They were arguing. Grace put on her helmet and flattened herself against the wall near the kitchen door, listening.

'All we need is another week!' begged Mrs Smew's voice. 'The new crop's selling ever so well at market. If you can wait till then we can give you the full amount—'

'You misunderstand,' the lower voice cut in. 'Waiting is not what I do. Being paid promptly and without excuses is what I do. Do you get what I'm driving at here, Mrs Smew? Do you divine my meaning?'

There was another bang and the sound of something shattering. It sounded to Grace like one of the many jars lining the kitchen shelves. Mrs Smew gave another shriek.

'Have mercy, Mr Helminth!' said Mrs Smew. 'Please! I don't know what else we can do when we simply don't have the money—'

Grace drew Swickstipe from her scabbard and stepped into the kitchen. A peculiar sight greeted her. A very tall man stood by the kitchen door. His skin was pale and his face was completely expressionless. On his head he wore a tall hat, the top of which was open like the lid of a pedal bin, and poking through it was a fat grey slug.

'Oh!' said the low voice, sounding amused. 'And who's this?'

It took Grace a moment to realise it was the slug who had spoken and not the man. The man wasn't even looking at her. He was staring ahead with the blank expression of a clothes shop mannequin.

Grace pointed Swickstipe at the slug. 'I have an idea. Why don't you turn around and walk out of here and then I won't have to spend half an hour cleaning bits of dead slug off my sword?'

The slug chuckled. 'Feisty, ain't she?'

The expression of the man wearing the hat remained blank.

Grace took a step towards them.

'Oh, don't get involved, love!' said Mrs Smew, wringing her hands. 'It's our problem. It's nothing to do with you. Run along now while you can.'

'You helped me,' said Grace. 'Seems only fair to offer a bit of help in return.'

'But you can't do anything. Not against Mr Helminth.'

Grace eyed the slug. Her lip curled. 'Doesn't look that tough to me.'

There was a flash of light and a loud bang. Grace felt herself hurled backwards against the wall of the kitchen. She slid to the floor and looked up, half-stunned, as the man in the hat strode towards her, his face still without emotion. Grace wondered if the slug was controlling him, using him as a kind of vehicle.

'Please don't upset Mr Helminth,' said Mrs Smew. 'He's a lightning slug. He can do terrible things.'

'Lightning slug?' muttered Grace as she clambered to her feet. She had heard of eels who could stun their prey with powerful static electric charges produced within their bodies, so why not slugs, too, she supposed?

'Indeed!' rasped the slug. 'So unless you want another thunderbolt – one a good deal more power-ful that will fry you to a cinder – I suggest you make yourself scarce.' He chuckled again.

Grace backed away from the man and the slug, Swickstipe still clutched in her fist. She found, to her great surprise and delight, that she had a plan. 'Leave this woman alone,' she said and raised the sword once more.

The man took a sidestep, keeping himself and the slug in line with Grace.

'Sorry, miss,' said the slug. 'There's money to be made on this farm and you aren't the one who's going to stop—'

With a rapid jerk of her forearm, Grace threw Swickstipe towards the slug. The slug ducked down inside the man's hat and the sword whistled over its slimy head.

'Oh dear!' said the slug, emerging from its hiding place. 'I do believe someone here is about to die rather horribly.'

'I agree,' said Grace. 'And it won't be me.'

'What – ugghhh!'

Grace's sword had pierced an earthenware jar high on a shelf above the slug. Cracked, the jar now burst open and poured its contents – a rough white granular substance – over the slug. Grace hoped the salt would have the same effect on Brokenshire slugs that it had on their Mainland cousins.

The slug made a horrid gargling noise as the man's hat filled up with the white grains. Grace could see the creature shrivelling to nothingness before her eyes. There was a small *phut* noise. A tiny wisp of black smoke erupted from the top of the man's hat and he pitched forward on to the floor. He sat up, blinking rapidly, the colour returning to his face.

'Gosh,' he said simply. He removed his hat and poured out a stream of white granules on to the kitchen floor. There appeared to be nothing left of the slug. He rubbed his head, confused, and looked up at Grace and Mrs Smew. 'What am I doing here?' he asked.

'You had a lightning slug in your hat,' explained Mrs Smew. 'It rode you around like a horse and cart for a bit but you'll be fine now.'

Grace picked up Swickstipe and wiped its blade clean on her gauntlet. 'Sorry about the jar,' she said to Mrs Smew. 'I guess you'll have to find something else to keep your salt in now.'

'Think nothing of it, love,' said Mrs Smew. 'And thank you! I wish I'd thought of that thing with the salt myself months ago! That damnable slug's been demanding money from us for nearly a year. I thought it would ruin us. There must be something I can do to thank you?'

'No need,' said Grace. 'I really need to go now and take this poultice to my friend.'

'Of course,' said Mrs Smew. 'But before you go, will you run to my bedroom – it's first on the left up the stairs – and fetch my headache pills off my dresser? They're in a little blue box. This chap here's bound to be feeling rotten after having that slug controlling his brain for who knows how long.'

'Sure thing.'

The farmhouse's staircase was narrow and covered in a black-and-white-checked carpet. Pictures of all sizes jostled for space on the walls, one of which was black, the other white. She paused to examine the black wall. One of the paintings showed a young man with the same long, thin nose and small curranty eyes as Mrs Smew. Below his portrait was a caption.

Albert Smew
Defeater of Thackeray Ross, Captain Bayleaf
and Owen Griffkin

The next portrait showed another young man with similar features. His caption identified him as:

Ross Smew
Defeater of Iris Oakthighs

There were portraits of three more young men, all sharing the same long nose and tiny, squinting eyes. The caption on the final one read:

Eustace Smew
Defeater of Grace of the Cave-of-the-Dandelion-Choir

Grace now looked at the opposite wall, which was painted white. There she found pictures of herself, Wellingtonia and other People of the Day. All were drawn in an unflattering, caricature style that gave them cruel, leering expressions. She felt a gnawing sensation in the pit of her stomach.

She carried on to the top of the stairs and stopped abruptly in her tracks, her heart suddenly booming like a gong when she saw the small framed picture hanging on the landing wall. In flowery embroidered letters it read:

Death to all People of the Day!

10

Four Things That Aren't Wood Pigeons

Back on the road, Grace coated the inside of a bandage with the pungent poultice Mrs Smew had prepared and tied it tightly around Jonathan's injured ankle. The big T. rex let out a long, hissing sigh, his thick tongue wriggling like a snake. He closed his eyes.

'Oof! That feels better already.'

'Mrs Smew said it was fast-acting but it's probably good to rest a bit longer,' said Grace.

'What was she like, this Mrs Smew?' asked Sarah.

Grace was wiping the leftover poultice from her hands. She didn't look up. What would be the point of letting her companions know that Mrs Smew was, for all practical purposes, their deadly enemy? 'Oh. She's a sweet old lady.'

They would see no sunset on their journey because no sun was ever visible in Brokenshire. Instead, as evening approached, the light simply began to ebb away from all directions. A sharp breeze rippled the grass beside the road.

On Wellingtonia's back, Grace drummed her fingers absently against the helmet tied to her belt. Inside her head, strange, disquieting thoughts were ricocheting like marbles.

Mrs Smew and her family were People of the Night! One of Mrs Smew's sons had personally defeated (did that mean killed?) one of the previous Graces! And yet Mrs Smew had been so kind to her. Was it because the old woman's eyesight was so bad she hadn't recognised Grace from the pictures on her own walls? Whatever her sons may have done, Mrs Smew herself was a good person, wasn't she? And yet the embroidered picture at the top of her stairs suggested otherwise.

Furthermore, Grace was now feeling a strange unease about sharing this information with the rest of her party. She suspected they wouldn't have been as kind to Mrs Smew as Grace had been, had they known which side of the Worthy War she was on.

'There. Can you hear it?' asked Sarah, cupping a hand to her ear.

Grace snapped out of her daydream. She could hear a steady, rushing, roaring sound.

'What is it?'

'Look, m'dears! Ahead! The Rat Tail River.'

They had arrived at the bank of a mighty, fast-flowing river, almost half a mile wide. Grace was astonished to finds its water was greyish-pink. It frothed and spumed violently around the jagged black rocks that pierced its surface like claws through flesh. Its long winding course and grey-pink colouring did indeed resemble the tail of some monstrous rat.

'From here we go north,' said Wellingtonia. 'We follow the river and that will bring us to the castle where the trigger wolf is being kept. It's not far. Stay alert because we are bound to run into the Elite Assassin Force of the People of the Night.'

'I'll protect us with one o' my Mid-Range Wood Pigeon Spells,' said Sarah. She muttered something unintelligible under her breath and clapped her hands together six times.

Not wanting to interrupt her, Grace nudged Jonathan. 'What's she doing?'

'Interacting with the magical air of Brokenshire. Using it to create a Mid-Range Wood Pigeon Spell.'

'And one of those is ... ?'

Sarah finished her ritual by twirling her index finger six times. 'It means, m'dear, that anyone looking at us from a distance of about thirty feet or more won't see us but will see four wood pigeons instead. It's a disguise. Should keep us safe for a while at least.'

Grace blinked, astonished – and then was even more astonished to find that when she blinked, Sarah,

Jonathan and Wellingtonia transformed briefly into three plump, purplish-grey wood pigeons. She looked down at her own hand, blinked, and for an instant it became the tip of a purplish-grey wing.

Sarah watched her, amused. 'I daresay magic takes a bit o' getting used to if you're a Mainlander.'

'This is a super cool skill to have,' said Grace. 'If I could do it, I'd disguise myself as a wood pigeon and do naughty things all over my brother's head when he's parading about on the rugby field.' She snorted with laughter and was surprised to feel a sudden odd pang, realising she was actually quite proud of her brother's sporting achievements. A weird thought occurred. She wasn't *missing* him, was she? No, of course not. She blinked, mentally changing the subject. 'How did you learn magic, Sarah?'

The sorceress stared into the distance, her long pink hair fluttering in the wind. 'I was a natural. Used to do nutty little spells when I was tiny like making spoons invisible and levitating buns. Never pursued it, though. When I was seven my ma and pa were killed in the Battle of the Fiery Pond and I have been raising my little brother, Jasper, on my own ever since. The hedgehog family next door are looking after him while I'm on this mission.'

'You lost your parents? Oh, Sarah.'

'Anyway,' continued Sarah. 'One day when he was four, Jasper got bitten by a tulip.'

'A tulip? The flower?'

'S'right.' Sarah nodded gravely. 'One of the deadliest of all flowers is the tulip. Magic in their poison, see? Get bit by one o' them critters and you fade away like a ghost until there's nothing left of you. Takes about a month for you to vanish completely and there's no known cure. Well, that's when I turned to magic. Went on a desperate crash course learnin' every type of magic I could to see if anything could help Jasper. Spent weeks in an enchantment camp building up my magical strength. Did eventually find a spell, as it happens. A ritual involving pencilflower and bogmoss. Brings him back when he starts to fade. But the effects aren't permanent. I have to carry out the ritual once a month or Jasper'd just evaporate like breath on a cold morning.'

In her mind, Grace pictured a young boy fading away to nothingness, a phantom unable to grasp so much as a rattle, let alone hug his sister. She shivered.

They followed the river, pausing after a few miles to pick some caramel berries from a sugar shrub and rest. After their meal, Grace stood up and strode off towards a clump of tall bushes, tugging at the straps that held her armour in place.

'Where are you going, child?' called Wellingtonia.

'Even saviours have to pee,' said Grace.

As she was suiting up again afterwards, her eye was caught by a silvery glint in the undergrowth. Once her armour was refastened securely, she investigated and found a large silver coin lying in a clump of thick grass. It was about twice the size of a ten-pence piece and carried a portrait of some stern-looking king wearing a heavy crown. As she stooped to retrieve it, the coin suddenly jumped into the air, seemingly of its own accord, and landed a few feet away in a patch of dried mud. Now it showed the reverse side, which featured a picture of a young woman fighting a skeleton. Grace bent to pick it up but once again, before she could reach it, the coin hurled itself into the air and plopped quietly on to the ground a short distance away.

This time Grace was determined to not let it escape. She crept up on the coin slowly, holding her breath, as if she were a collector stalking some rare and precious butterfly. Hands cupped, she knelt down carefully beside the coin and ...

... before she could slam her palms together, the coin flew into the air and tinkled to the ground on a stony patch of earth a little way off near the entrance to a small wooded glade.

One more go, thought Grace. *One more and that's it.*

Armour clanking, she sank to the ground and crawled on her tummy, slow and snake-like, towards the silver coin. Night was fast approaching and the light was fading quickly now. The gleaming coin looked like a single bright star in a dull night sky. With slow, patient movements, she approached her prey and raised a gauntleted hand ...

... but again, infuriatingly, like a fly that

stubbornly refuses to be swatted, the coin leaped into the air. Grace sprang to her feet, tracking the coin's trajectory with her eyes – and saw it drop neatly into the outstretched palm of a heavily built bald man wearing long dark robes. In his other hand, he carried a gleaming broad-bladed hatchet.

'The self-flipping coin,' crooned the man in a low, silky voice, dropping the coin into his pocket. Her gazed at her like a fox at a chicken dinner. 'Such a simple invention and yet so effective at separating a single animal from the flock. How very pleasant it is to see your face again, Grace, although I had rather imagined our previous meeting would be our final one.'

'What do you mean?' said Grace. She backed away slowly, casting a quick glance around for the others. There was no sign of them. 'We've never met before.'

The man's thick eyebrows hoisted themselves halfway up his forehead. 'Have we not met, then? Well, goodness me! That means you must be Grace number fifteen and the Worthy War has not long to play out! How splendid! In that case, I feel an introduction is in order, is it not?' The man cleared his throat theatrically. 'Grace number fifteen, allow me to introduce myself. My name is Cardinal Axminster of the People of the Night and I am going to kill you.'

11

A Large Man and a Small Bird

Grace backed away faster. She reached for the scabbard hanging from her armour and wrenched out Swickstipe. She licked her lips, which felt dry and scratchy as sandpaper. Her hand trembled. Was she actually going to fight this man in single combat? Hadn't the previous Grace mentioned she'd injured him? Perhaps he was weakened, hiding wounds beneath his black robes?

With a vicious leer, Cardinal Axminster lunged forward, swiping his heavy hatchet through the air with a low swishing sound. 'Pertle the Pious Poet prophesied one of us People of the Night would be your defeater. I had no inkling the honour would fall to me!'

'How did you even find us?' she demanded. 'We were magically disguised as wood pigeons.'

'Ha! Yes. Funny story, actually. I mistook you for a wood pigeon I know called Rod Petheridge. Blighter owes me ten gold coins I won from him at cards. Been after him for months. Only, when I get close, he starts shimmering and turns into a young girl. And bless my soul if it isn't an actual Grace!' He slashed the hatchet through the air again. Grace felt the breeze against her cheek. 'Next time you might want to disguise yourself as a creature less likely to run up gambling debts. Except, of course,' he sniggered, 'there won't *be* a next time because, as I believe I mentioned earlier, I am going to kill you.' He laughed loudly.

Grace waved Swickstipe and tried to make her face look fierce. 'Oh yeah?' she called. Her voice sounded small and pathetically childish to her own ears. 'Well, maybe you're not going to do that. Actually. Maybe I'm going to be the one who—'

KLANKK!

With a swift swish of his hatchet, Cardinal Axminster knocked Swickstipe from Grace's hand. The sword flew through the air and impaled itself into the trunk of a nearby tree.

'Please,' said Cardinal Axminster with a sickly smile, 'do go on. You were saying?'

'Yeah, well. Maybe I was wrong about that,' laughed Grace nervously. Behind her she could hear the roar of the Rat Tail River. Or was it simply the sound of her own blood pounding in her ears? 'Can't we talk about this? Do you actually *need* to chop me up with that thing?'

'Oh, I'm afraid so,' said Cardinal Axminster gravely. 'You see, if I chop you up into little bits then you'll be less likely to defeat our Fearsome Foe. And as I don't want anyone to do that ...' He slashed the hatchet through the air again. 'Chop chop it has to be. I'm awfully sorry, but there we have it, old girl.'

'Look,' she said, hands raised. 'All I know is – eek!'

She hadn't intended to utter this last word. It

was squeezed out of her quite involuntarily by the sheer terror of finding the ground vanish beneath her feet as she stepped backwards. Heart drumming, she flailed a hand and snatched hold of a tree root protruding from the riverbank. Below her, the pinky-grey water of the Rat Tail River churned and frothed over vicious black rocks. She groaned and tried to haul herself back up.

The hairless dome of Cardinal Axminster's head appeared over the edge of the riverbank, his pale, doughy face a mask of pure malice. Bending down to Grace with a low chuckle of triumph, he raised the hatchet over her wrist.

'And this, alas,' he crooned, 'must be where you and I part company. And where, sadly, you must apparently part company with your hand. Forgive me, young Grace. I do not inflict pain for the sake of my own pleasure. That is merely a side effect. I do this because it is the right thing to do. For centuries, we People of the Night have fought the terror and cruel injustices inflicted by you evil People of the Day, and now …'

Grace caught a brief glimpse of a thick scaly tail

thrashing through the air like a whip and heard a deafening crash as it slammed into Cardinal Axminster, sending him reeling, his heavy hatchet clanging to the ground.

'Jonathan?'

Now the T. rex's scaly head came into view over the edge of the riverbank. 'Can't we leave you alone for five minutes without you getting into trouble?'

He lowered his tail to Grace and she grasped tightly on to the thick scales. With one deft flick, the dinosaur pulled her up and deposited her on the riverbank. She heard the sound of hoofs and saw Wellingtonia galloping in their direction with Sarah on her back.

'Thanks, JV. Where did the Cardinal go?' With a grunt, she pulled Swickstipe from the tree trunk it had lodged in and slid it back into its scabbard.

With his single arm, Jonathan pointed at where the stunned Cardinal was hauling himself painfully to his feet near the entrance to the wood. He cast one look at the two of them, swiped up his hatchet from the ground and dashed into the forest.

'I don't suppose we'll be seeing him again,' said

Grace. 'You scared him off good and proper.'

There was a rustling sound and several menacing shapes loomed at them from the dark wood.

'Probably not,' agreed Jonathan, 'but it looks like we will be seeing the other members of the Elite Assassin Force he just set on us.'

Wellingtonia and Sarah arrived. 'Grace, m'dear,' said Sarah, climbing down from Wellingtonia's saddle. 'What did we miss?'

'You missed me nearly being killed,' said Grace, 'but it's OK because you've arrived just in time to see all four of us be killed by whatever unknown horrors are about to lurch out of that forest.'

'Oh, that's no problem,' said Sarah with a wink. 'I eat unknown horrors for breakfast.'

Four shapes now stepped from the trees and confronted them. They differed greatly in shape and size but all seemed to share the same deadly intent.

Grace's hand slid back to the hilt of her sword. 'What *are* they?'

'Well,' said Jonathan, 'the big one with pointy ears is a venom goblin. The small grey thing with

wings is a slate dragon. The chap with the long nose and stripy face is a badger knight.'

'And the tiny yellow thing that looks like a chick?'

'It's a chick,' said Jonathan. 'A rubefaction chick. I'd be very, very careful of it.'

'A ruby-what?'

But before he could answer, the venom goblin cut him off with a sneering, inhuman laugh. 'This is a restricted area!' it growled. 'The penalty for trespassing is death in the style of my choosing. And I choose *very nasty indeed*.'

The four creatures sprang at them, weapons raised, screeching battle cries.

Its small green eyes blazing, the venom

goblin charged at Jonathan, sword slashing. Jonathan bared his enormous teeth, fending off each blow with flicks of his tail.

The badger knight bowled towards Wellingtonia. It preened its long, moustache-like whiskers. 'Tired old nag! You'll make a fine horsemeat stew when I'm finished with you!'

The slate dragon buzzed around Sarah's head. Its wings made a dry creaking sound like the door of an ancient tomb. 'I trust my lady likes her eggs hard-boiled,' it burbled and began to drop a stream of heavy egg-shaped rocks.

The tiny yellow thing waddled towards Grace on two short spindly legs. With the tip of one tiny stumpy wing, it clutched a miniature sword the size of a matchstick.

Grace couldn't help but laugh. The creature looked like something attached to a key ring you won from a machine in an arcade. But her experiences so far in Brokenshire suggested there would be more to this animal than met the eye. What had Jonathan called it? A *rubefaction chick*? What did that even mean? She'd never heard the word before.

With much puffing and panting, the tiny chick clambered up a rock until it was at Grace's eye level. Grace unsheathed Swickstipe and pointed it straight at the chick's head.

'I don't want any trouble out of you, pipsqueak,' she told the tiny bird. 'You can see I've got this enormous sword and I could slice you in two, easy peasy. So just stay there until this battle's over and I'll let you leave in one piece. That sound OK?'

'Oh, Grace,' said the chick. Its voice was surprisingly deep and adult sounding. It reminded Grace of the voice on her mum's relaxation playlist that told you to imagine you were lying on a Mediterranean beach and let your cares float away. 'What are you doing?'

'What am I doing?' Grace gave a snort. 'Well, if it's any of your business, titch, I'm on my way to save the entire county of Brokenshire from death and destruction, actually. I'm the Fifteenth and Final Grace. The saviour. Pretty flipping important job, some might say.'

'No, not that,' said the chick patiently. 'Obviously you'll fail at that because you're a twelve-year-old

Mainlander with no experience of warfare, whatever the prophecies might say. I mean what are you doing with your life in general?'

'My life in general?' Grace cocked her head to one side and folded her arms. 'Sorry, I don't follow.'

'Well,' said the chick, 'if I can speak frankly, you seem to be making a fair old mess of it, don't you?'

'Oh, I do, do I?' retorted Grace. It wasn't much of a retort but the chick had caught her off guard and it was all she could think of.

'Oh, most definitely,' continued the chick. 'Let's see. You cheated in your Geography test by writing the capitals of all European countries on the inside of your pencil case. At the last count you've told three different girls in your class that they're your number one absolute best friend simply to get birthday presents out of them. Only last week you dropped one of your mother's best earrings down the bathroom sink and have yet to tell her about it ...'

With each of these accusations, Grace's face began to glow with a tremendous surge of heat. Realising she was blushing, she rubbed her cheeks and glared at the chick. 'How do you even know these things about me?'

The chick ignored her question. 'The real reason your pet hamster Jiggles died was because you accidentally dropped him on the kitchen floor when you were flying him around like Superman and not from "a disease of the inner ear" as you later told your parents ...'

A wave of fire seemed to pass through Grace's entire body. 'Shut up!' she demanded. 'Shut up!'

'When you were five you stole the last slice of Lucy Prebble's birthday cake and blamed it on her dog, which was then hit on the nose with a newspaper by Lucy's dad and locked in the yard with no food for a whole day. When you were six you threw a tangerine at an old lady who had told you off for dropping litter on a school trip to Chester Zoo. When you were seven you sneezed in the school library's only copy of *The Wind in the Willows* and simply closed the book and put it back on the shelf. When you were ...'

'I said shut up!' yelled Grace, her voice strained and breathless. The heat she felt was almost overpowering now. It was like she was being boiled alive inside her armour. 'I didn't *mean* to do any of those things! Not really!'

'... eight,' continued the chick, 'you tied Mason Merriman's shoelaces together after he drew attention to the fact that you're not very good at colouring in, causing him to fall over in the playground and break his cheekbone. You falsely claimed you had tied his laces because one was loose and you didn't want him to trip up, and that you had no idea how the lace of one shoe became entwined with the other. You even, I believe, went as far as claiming, that maybe some "naughty pixie or elf" had committed the act, thereafter giving Mason months of nightmares about evil pixies and elves. You did all this, Grace, didn't you?'

'It was all just stupid kid stuff!' panted Grace, her face flushed and scarlet. 'I never meant any actual *harm*. Please stop now. Point taken!'

'When you were nine ...'

'I said stop!' Grace jabbed clumsily at the chick with Swickstipe. Her limbs felt as if she had sunburn and were almost too painful to move. The tiny bird dodged the blow effortlessly and continued talking in its deep voice.

'When you were nine your brother, James, won a book token in a spelling contest and in an act of jealousy you broke every single one of his pencils.'

This last wave of heat seemed to affect Grace more than all the previous ones combined. Gasping, she slumped to the ground, feeling like a potato inside a microwave oven. The chick jumped off the rock, its stumpy wings fluttering furiously, and landed gently on Grace's tummy. Slowly, it began to waddle towards her face.

'You think that was bad, Grace? That was the tip of the iceberg. I've found dozens of memories like that about your brother inside your head. Dozens and dozens. Would you like to hear some more? I know a great one about a guitar.'

12

Rubefaction

Sarah was dodging the hail of rock eggs. Screeching, the slate dragon banked sharply over her head and returned for another assault.

The sorceress muttered quietly to herself and clapped her hands together twice.

'I think someone needs a time-out.'

The slate dragon froze in mid-air, a stream of rock eggs halfway towards the ground.

Nearby, Jonathan and the venom goblin were engaged in vicious combat. 'I've heard about you, *Jonathan Vetchling*,' sneered the venom goblin.

'Have you indeed? How fascinating?' replied

Jonathan in a bored voice.

'Yeah,' it continued, 'a Tyrannosaurus rex that doesn't eat meat! Bit of a joke, really, aren't you, mate? A bet all the other dinosaurs have a giggle about you behind your back.'

'For your information,' said Jonathan, 'I think you'll find my parties are the best attended in this part of the county, people flock from far and wide to ask for my recipe for vegan lemon cheesecake and my book group is so popular we've had to move it to a bigger venue.'

'Book group?' The venom goblin paused, its lipless mouth hanging open. 'Huh. Wish we had time for such things in the Elite Assassin Force.'

'You should come along,' said Jonathan. 'We meet on the last Thursday of every month. I usually lay on a vegan cream tea afterwards.'

'Really?' said the venom goblin, lowering its sword. A small, hopeful smile softened its harsh features.

'No!' laughed Jonathan. 'You're an evil monster who's trying to kill me. Of course I'm not going to invite you to join my book group.'

Before the venom goblin could reply, Jonathan slammed his thick scaly tail down on the creature's head.

A short distance away, the badger knight had cornered Wellingtonia between a large wall of rock and the edge of the riverbank.

'Your doom is at hand, lady horse,' it said, its whiskery moustache twitching, 'but fear not. I shall tell the whole county how bravely you fought and with what reluctance I was finally forced to end your—'

He got no further because at that moment Wellingtonia planted a savage kick in the middle of his chest that sent him sailing through the air in a long, graceful arc. He plummeted with a soft splash into the middle of the Rat Tail River and was swept out of sight by the powerful current.

Meanwhile, the rubefaction chick was standing on the breastplate of Grace's armour and staring straight at her with its two tiny blank eyes. Grace could barely make it out because her eyes were swimming with scalding tears.

'This guitar business,' it said. 'It's a real shocker

of a tale. You claim it was an accident but I think deep down inside yourself you might think something else ...'

'Be quiet!' she yelled. 'I don't want to listen to all this stuff! I can't take it! It's burning me up!'

'Perhaps you suspected you were about to stand on his guitar but in your mind you thought you could plausibly claim to have made an honest mistake ...'

She clamped her gauntleted hands over her ears but it was no good. The chick's voice seemed to be broadcasting inside her head. Maybe if she put on her helmet it might block out the chick's power? Like the way the radio in the family car went silent when they drove under a concrete bridge that blocked out the signal. Then another idea occurred.

As fast as she could, she untied her helmet from her belt and slammed it over the chick, trapping it against the breastplate of her armour like a spider under a cup. Immediately, the awful heat coursing through her body began to diminish. Holding the helmet firmly against the breastplate, she clambered to her feet and sat down on a tree stump, filling her scalded lungs with cool evening air. Tears ran down her armour like raindrops. With her free hand, she wiped the corners of her eyes.

Inside the helmet, the rubefaction chick was still talking, its voice muffled and metallic-sounding. Grace craned her neck forward to listen.

'Just after you hatched you pecked your sister's foot when she accidentally trod on your wing, making her cry. You forgot to send your mother a birthday card, claiming to be too busy training with the Army of the People of the Night, but the truth was you couldn't be bothered. You stole Rowan Snipwell's best penknife and claimed you'd seen it fall into the Sulphurous Meadow of Haralbert ...'

Using her teeth, Grace pulled off a gauntlet and felt the side of her helmet. It was almost too hot to touch. A faint aroma of roasting chicken wafted at her through its eyeholes. *The chick was cooking itself.*

She lifted the helmet a crack and the chick plopped out on to the ground, its coat of yellow fuzz blackened, a plume of steam rising from its tiny head. Quick as a mouse, it scuttled to the riverbank on its spindly legs and dived headlong into the rushing waters. There was a loud hissing sound as the seething current carried it away out of sight.

'They make fearsome opponents, rubefaction chicks,' said Jonathan, joining her on the riverbank. 'They act like a kind of shame funnel. *Rubefaction* means to make something red. And that's what they do. Remind you of every shameful thing you've ever done until you blush yourself to death. Terrific idea to trap it inside your helmet. It had nothing to shame but its own reflection.'

Grace sat down heavily, her armour clanking. She rubbed her eyes.

Oh, Grace, you idiot. She had been a terrible sister. Was still a terrible sister. Jealous. Spiteful. Thoroughly selfish. James had never once been anything other than a good brother to her. She realised how much she loved him and how hard she had tried to squash down that feeling of love whenever he succeeded at stuff, because her own achievements were so pathetic by comparison. Her stomach felt like it was full of stones. She wished he was here with her now to help with this terrible task she was facing. He would know what to do.

'Are we all here, all alive and well?' called Sarah.

'Yes,' said Wellingtonia.

'Yes,' said Jonathan.

'Yes,' said Grace. 'Slightly to my surprise.' She clambered to her feet.

'Well done, all,' said Sarah. 'Now, let's move quickly. Be just our luck if there're more o' them Elite Assassin types lurking around here.'

As they were setting off along the riverbank again, a peal of dry, creaking laughter erupted over their heads. They turned to see the slate dragon whooshing towards them, its eyes blazing with malice. Jonathan raised his sword.

'Confound the thing!' cried Sarah. 'I wish I could make my time-out spells last a bit longer.'

Burbling maniacally, the slate dragon swooped over their heads and breathed a sizzling torrent of white fire at Sarah. The sorceress caught the full force of the blast and slumped to the ground. With a clatter of its stony wings, the slate dragon soared away into the distance, vanishing into the darkening sky.

Grace dashed to help Sarah. The white fire didn't seem to have burned her at all or even singed her clothes. She sat up and stared at Grace woozily.

'Are you OK?'

Sarah blinked, dazed. 'No harm done that I can make out.' She suddenly gasped. 'Oh my good flippin' gracious. Oh my sweet stars! You know what that was, don't you?'

'A slate dragon, wasn't it?'

'Not the dragon,' said Sarah. 'That fire it breathed. It was the Terrible White Fire of Winter-Cress!'

'What was so terrible about it?' asked Grace. 'You seem fine.'

Sarah held out her hands and stared at them sadly. 'I ain't. The Terrible White Fire of Winter-Cress breaks a person's connection with the magical air of Brokenshire. I've lost my magical powers!'

They made their way north along the bank of the Rat Tail River.

Trudging along next to Grace, Sarah kicked at a stone moodily. 'How am I going to carry out my

Jasper's monthly ritual now with no magic powers? He'll fade away to nothing. Oh, I'm a terrible sister.'

'You're a fantastic sister,' said Grace. 'And I should know because I'm the world's worst. There must be a way to get your powers back. And even if there isn't there must be someone in the whole of this county who can help Jasper.'

'Maybe. But I feel so useless, Grace. What's a sorceress without magic? Nothin', that's what.'

'I'll tell you what a sorceress without magic is,' said Grace. 'A person. Just like me. Is that so awful?'

'But you're special,' said Sarah. 'You're the Fifteenth and Final Grace.'

'I'm just some random who wanted to avoid a bunch of trouble at home. I'm

about as un-special as it gets.'

'But you were born to save us all.'

'So your song-singer bloke reckons. Nothing to do with me.'

Before long, a tall, narrow building came into view. It reminded Grace of a chess piece. What were they called? Ravens? Crows? Rooks. Probably rooks. The castle-y ones, anyway. Its slender battlements were streaked with ivy and crumbling with age. Outside, illuminated by the flickering light of several fiery torches, stood a ring of guards, a mixture of humans and other creatures.

Grace and the others hid behind a rocky outcropping on the riverbank.

'Well,' said Wellingtonia, 'this is the place we need to get inside. If anyone has any great ideas about how we can achieve this, now would be the ideal time to share them with the rest of the group.'

13

Connections

'I had been plannin' on usin' my magic to put all them guards in a time-out and then reach out with my mind to find the trigger wolf,' said Sarah, her eyes downcast, 'but that won't be happenin' now I lost my connection to the air.'

The word 'connection' reverberated in Grace's mind. She slid off her frog-shaped backpack and rummaged inside. 'This magical air you have here. How does it work exactly?'

Sarah shrugged. 'Well, it's like the air is full of songs and stories and information about anythin' you want. And there's all these useful things it can do if you know how to ask it.'

'We have something like that on the Mainland,' said Grace. 'We call it the internet.'

From inside the bag she drew out a small black rectangular slab.

'What's that? A bar o' chocolate?'

'It's my phone,' said Grace. 'It's how you connect with the magical air of the Mainland. I wonder if it'll work here ... ?' She swiped her finger across its surface and the screen lit up, displaying a grid of coloured squares. 'These are the apps,' explained Grace. 'They let you do useful things.' She frowned. 'Hang on. These aren't my apps. They've all changed. *Spell of Summoning, Spell of Visions* ... All the apps on my phone have turned into magic spells!'

'That's the Brokenshire air!' said Sarah excitedly. 'It gets into everythin'. I 'spect it's converted your phone to work here.'

Grace touched the *Spell of Visions* icon. A map not unlike the one Mary had shown them at Jonathan's house suddenly appeared, glowing in the air above the phone. By touching the projection, she was able to zoom in on the image. Soon she had found the castle and was examining a detailed layout of its rooms.

'Happy days!' said Grace. 'I could kick myself for not checking my phone earlier.'

''Ow marvellous!' said Sarah. 'You *are* able to do magic after all. Can you teach me how to use one o' these phone gizmos?'

'No probs,' said Grace. 'It's not hard. The main thing you need is parents to pay the bill. Anyway, look *here* ...' She pointed to a large chamber below ground level. 'The dungeon. Looks about the only place big enough and strong enough to stand any chance of holding a trigger wolf if it got angry. And see here? There's a handy passage leading right to it from the outside.'

'Then our task is simple,' said Wellingtonia. 'If Grace can use this phone contraption to freeze the guards in a time-out, we can sneak into the castle through the passage and retrieve the trigger wolf. We will of course have to be extremely careful not to upset or anger the beast in the slightest.'

'Leave that to me,' said Grace. 'I'm a dog person.'

'A dog person?' repeated Wellingtonia, shocked. 'Like a werewolf, you mean?'

'No, it just means I like dogs and they like me,' said Grace, rolling her eyes. 'On the Mainland people often prefer either cats or dogs.'

'Seems rather prejudiced,' said Wellingtonia.

'Sorry for interruptin',' said Sarah. 'But what does "one per cent battery remaining" mean?'

'Aw, what?'

The map of the dungeon suddenly melted into the air and the phone's screen went black.

'Fudgecakes,' muttered Grace. 'It's died on us. Stupid thing.' She felt a powerful urge to sling the useless item away as hard as she could but restrained herself.

Jonathan put his hand on Grace's shoulder. 'That poor little creature. Its sacrifice shall not be in vain.'

'It's not *dead* dead,' said Grace. 'I just mean it's out of power. We're magic-less again. What now?'

Wellingtonia shook her long head in the equine equivalent of a shrug, rippling her long mane. 'The plan must proceed. We must steal the trigger wolf. We have no other option.'

'Sarah and I will draw the guards away as best we can,' said Jonathan. 'We'll try to lead them into the woods behind the castle. Then you and Grace should be able to get into the passage down to the dungeon.'

'And how do you suggest we get the trigger wolf out without it destroying everything?' asked Wellingtonia.

'Other than "with extreme care", I can't help you with that,' said Jonathan.

'Didn't think so,' said Grace. 'But I'm sure it'll all go without a hitch and be extremely safe.'

'You reckon?' said Sarah.

'Well, a little mindless optimism can't hurt, can it?'

Sarah nudged Jonathan. 'Right, you big lizard. Let's give 'em their chance.'

'Good luck,' said Grace.

'To you an' all, m'dears,' said Sarah and with a nod, she and Jonathan slipped away into the evening gloom.

'I wish I was as brave as that pair,' muttered Grace.

'Don't be too hard on yourself,' said Wellingtonia. 'In the short time I've known you, you've gone from an enormous disappointment to merely a quite large disappointment.'

'Cheers, mate.' Grace straightened her armour and tightened the frog-shaped backpack around her shoulders. As she did so a memory came to her: it was James who had given her this backpack. Originally, it had been a present from their uncle Gareth at James's last birthday party but James had seen how much his sister admired it – Jim the frog was her favourite cartoon character after all – that he'd given it to her there and then. Funny. She'd completely forgotten that. She felt another pang of guilt for how she'd behaved towards her brother.

From behind the rocks, they watched as Sarah and Jonathan approached the castle. To their right lay the river, to their left a thick, knotty forest. Ahead, ringing the castle, stood the guards from the Elite Assassin Force.

'Good evenin', you clutch of absolute losers!' they heard Sarah call. 'Soldiers, are you? You're rubbish! I seen better soldiers sticking out o' the top o' boiled eggs!'

'I am forced to agree!' shouted Jonathan. 'You chaps are a frightful bunch! Scarlett Moss ought to be thoroughly ashamed of herself for engaging such a bedraggled bunch of misfits to guard this facility!'

'Trespassers,' muttered one guard lightly.

'Cheeky ones, too,' said another.

They drew their weapons.

Jonathan and Sarah turned and raced towards the forest. The guards pursued them.

Once the guards were a safe distance away, Grace clambered on to Wellingtonia's back and they sped towards the castle. They arrived at a small stone archway with a wooden door set into the rear of the building. Grace dismounted and gave the door a push. It didn't budge.

'Don't suppose you know any horsey magic spells for opening unlocked doors?' asked Grace hopefully.

Wellingtonia struck the door sharply with her hoof. There was a brief sound of crunching metal and the door swung open.

'Never really needed any, child.'

Within they found a wide stone staircase that spiralled downwards into blackness. Gingerly, they descended. Wellingtonia made sure to place down each of her hoofs with extreme care to ensure they didn't clatter noisily against the stone steps. After a while, the staircase levelled out into a gallery lit by flaming torches. It looked down into a dank, gloomy room where shadows flickered and danced on the damp walls. At its centre stood a tiny, fluffy wolf cub noisily lapping water from a bowl. Beside the cub stood a young dapple-grey horse. A mare.

Wellingtonia stared at her. She gave a snort of sadness, her big nostrils flaring. 'Olive Willow,' she whispered.

A fly buzzed around the cub's head. The cub snarled irritably and snapped its jaws at the insect. There was a strange noise like the crackling of an immense fire and suddenly the cub expanded like a balloon, quadrupling in size until it was as big as a fully grown wolf. The creature's snarling became a thundering rumble that echoed around the dismal dungeon.

The young mare, Olive Willow, wore a strange leather harness around her neck, something like a horse's nosebag, only instead of a bag containing oats, it held a huge conch shell a few inches from her mouth. It made Grace think of the wire holder for a harmonica that folk guitarists sometimes wore around their necks. She watched as Olive Willow stretched her neck forward and blew into this conch shell, emitting a low, pleasing note that reminded Grace of a church organ. It was like something else too – but she couldn't quite remember what …

The oversized wolf cub's ears pricked up. The snarling ceased. Once more, there was a sound like a crackling fire and the cub shrank back to its normal size.

'Good girl,' cooed Olive Willow to the cub. 'Who's a good girl, eh? That's right. Take it easy …'

'The sound of the shell controls the trigger wolf,' whispered Grace. 'We've got to get our hands on that somehow.'

'I'm sure you do,' said a high voice behind them.

They spun around to find a large, grinning, gingery bat hovering silently in the air a few feet above their heads. It was flanked by five burly guards holding swords and spears.

'Scarlett Moss,' breathed Wellingtonia.

'I knew this day would come,' trilled the bat. 'Like so much else it was foretold in the poems of Pertle the Pious Poet. It is inevitable that we People of the Night must triumph in the Worthy War. And by putting an end to your flimsy scheme to steal the trigger wolf, our glorious victory grows one step closer.'

'Very big on prophecies in this county, aren't you?' muttered Grace.

'Mum? Is that you?' called Olive Willow in astonishment and raced up the stairs to join them, her hoofs clacking loudly against the stone steps.

'It is,' said Wellingtonia levelly. Grace could tell she was trying to keep her emotions in check.

Olive Willow glared at her. 'Oh, Mum! Have you any idea how embarrassing it is to have a parent who's on the wrong side of the Worthy War? Why can't you ditch these evil ways of yours?'

'Evil ways of *mine?*' snorted Wellingtonia.

'You're the one who broke my heart by leaving home to join the People of the Night.'

'The People of the Night are *good*!' piped up Scarlett Moss. She fluttered on to a ledge and crossed her wings defiantly. 'It's you People of the Day who are the wicked ones. You hate everything we stand for.'

'We only hate you because you hate everything *we* stand for!' retorted Wellingtonia. 'Soros the Scared Song Singer is clear on that fact.'

'*No sane person believes a word they say*,' intoned Scarlett. '*Those vile, untruthful People of the Day*. The words of Pertle the Pious Poet. Words to live by.'

'All this bickering and nastiness,' said Grace. 'You both need to take a look at yourselves. Ever hear the expression six of one and half a dozen of the other?'

'I am aware of the expression,' said Scarlett. 'It means don't forget to blow out your candles before you go to sleep. I fail to see its relevance here.'

'That's not what *six of one and half a dozen of the other* means,' snorted Wellingtonia. 'The phrase is a reminder that the clocks go forward in spring.'

'Guys,' said Grace, 'it means both sides of the argument are equally at fault, so why not stop squabbling and get along with each other? Huh? Isn't that better than what you're doing now?'

'Don't be absurd, child,' said Wellingtonia coldly. 'The Worthy War must be fought. The People of the Night must be defeated.'

'Get along with the People of the Day?' hooted Scarlett. 'I'd rather die than be allied to those monsters!'

'We are *not* the monsters,' insisted Wellingtonia. 'You are. Which is why it's so hard to think of my own daughter wanting to side with you.'

'Ha! Typical People of the Day claptrap.' Scarlett was bellowing now, her words echoing off the stone walls. 'Why are you all so filled with hate?'

There came a loud snarl. Everyone gulped and stared down into the dungeon, where the trigger wolf cub had once again begun to grow rapidly in size.

'Quickly, Olive Willow!' shouted Scarlett. 'Blow the Calming Conch!'

Grace made a dash towards the young horse.

The young mare put her mouth to the conch

shell but before she could blow through it, Grace
unhooked it from its wire holder and held it aloft.

'I've got it!' cried Grace. 'And guess what,
Brokenshire people? That means I'm in charge!'

She had done it. She had found a way to end their war.
She. Clumsy, mediocre old Grace Parker. Her blood sang
with victory.

She took a deep breath and raised the conch to
her lips – but then the shiny shell slipped from her
grasp like a wet bar of soap and crashed to the stone
floor, shattering into thousands of tiny pieces.

Everyone stared at her in silent horror.

'Oops,' said Grace. 'My bad.'

14

Dog Tired

Faster and faster, larger and larger. The trigger wolf was ballooning at a terrifying pace. Its black-lipped jaws opened and it let out a snarl that shook the walls of the castle.

Grace, Wellingtonia, Scarlett and Olive Willow raced up the spiral staircase and out into the twilight in time to see the trigger wolf, now the size of a house, burst through the wall of the dungeon. Huge chunks of masonry rained down, sending everyone fleeing for the safety of the forest. The beast's head bobbed one way and then another, as if it was sniffing the air, before the animal hurtled away in the

direction of some dim lights in the distance, its thick tail wagging like a great pendulum.

'That's Crumblechester it's heading for, isn't it?' said Grace.

'Not for much longer it won't be,' sighed Scarlett Moss. 'These creatures' instinct is to cause havoc and destruction.'

'Isn't that what you wanted?'

'All we wanted was for it to break down the city's inner wall so our troops could get in and take control of the Governor's Palace. Once the wall was down we would have returned the trigger wolf to its harmless state with the Calming Conch. We didn't want to hurt anyone or cause unnecessary damage.'

Grace felt her face flushing. The rubefaction chick could have a field day with this memory. 'I've sort of ruined everything for everyone, haven't I?'

'Sort of?'

'Well, maybe a bit more than that.'

'You stupid, ignorant Mainlander child!' cried Wellingtonia. 'Our one hope of controlling that animal – and you destroyed it!'

'You blundering moron!' trilled Scarlett.

'You've royally messed up!'

'Oh,' said Grace, 'so you two finally agree on something, do you?'

Scarlet summoned a guard. 'Arrest her!'

'With great pleasure, ma'am,' growled a burly venom goblin, striding forward with an expression of cruel glee on its gnarled grey face.

Instinctively, Grace drew Swickstipe from its scabbard. *Finally, I'm getting the hang of this stuff*, she mused. *When it's ever so slightly too late.* The silvery blade flashed, its inscription faintly visible in the dim light.

OWWWWWWWWWWWWW ...

She thought of the dodo Petronilla Saxifrage. And then another thought dropped into Grace's mind. A bright shining star of a thought.

'Wait!' she demanded, holding up her hands. So authoritative did she sound that the venom goblin halted confusedly in its tracks. 'I know how to stop the trigger wolf! I can do it! Trust me!'

'Oh, *now* you do?' said Scarlett. 'Great timing, kid.'

*   *   *

Grace had a little expedition in mind.

Olive Willow led her and Wellingtonia down some stone steps to the river where a large raft made of thick tree trunks was tied to a post on the swirling grey-pink water.

'I had this moored here in case of emergencies,' said Olive Willow.

'Perfect,' said Grace. 'And the river flows so fast that with any luck we can be in Crumblechester before the trigger wolf arrives.'

Wellingtonia tested the sturdiness of the raft with her hoof. 'I'm sceptical of the soundness of your plan, Grace, your competence to carry it out, and the ability of this raft to take my weight.'

'But otherwise, you're cool with everything?'

Wellingtonia snorted and clambered aboard the raft. It rocked a little but held steady. Grace jumped aboard and began to untie the rope securing it to the post.

'Olive Willow. Once we're free can you give us a push?'

'Of course, Mum. Safe journey, yeah? I hope your plan works.'

'Thank you for helping us, Olive Willow,' said Wellingtonia. 'It's done my heart good to see you again.'

'If we can make up then why not all the People of the Night and the People of the Day?'

The two horses rubbed noses. Then Olive Willow placed her hoof on the edge of the raft and gave a mighty push. The wooden craft surged swiftly away on the frothing pink waters of the Rat Tail River.

In the forest, Sarah and Jonathan were in trouble. They had evaded the Elite Assassin Force for as long as they were able but now they were surrounded and hopelessly outnumbered. In whatever direction they turned, men and women brandishing swords and axes, vicious venom goblins, cruel snow beavers, sinister scorpion voles and a dozen other creatures were advancing on them with bloodthirsty leers.

'What I wouldn't give for just the teeniest morsel o' magic right now,' muttered Sarah.

'Stop!' trilled a voice. 'Elite Assassin Force, lower weapons and fall back!'

Everyone stared upwards in the direction from which the voice had come.

Scarlett Moss hovered overhead. 'Change of plan.'

Olive Willow's wooden raft bobbed and bounced along the thrashing water at tremendous speed. It was all Grace could do to cling to one of Wellingtonia's legs as the craft was whirled along like a cork, narrowly avoiding the jagged black rocks protruding like fangs through the swirling pink foam.

'And you're absolutely sure you can stop this trigger wolf using just your sword?' said Wellingtonia.

'Stop asking me that,' said Grace. 'You're making me doubt my own plan. I'd describe my overall level of sureness as *quite sure* to *pretty sure*, OK?'

Soon, the spires of a city were visible on the riverbank ahead, a mass of yellow lights glimmering in their windows. And rampaging towards them with mindless savagery along the bank was the vast bulk of the trigger wolf. Faint screams drifted on the air.

'It's almost reached the walls,' said Grace. 'We're not going to get there in time.'

There was a distant crash and the sound of falling rubble. A cloud of dust billowed over the city.

'It's broken through,' said Wellingtonia.

Grace hauled herself up into Wellingtonia's saddle. 'Can you make it to the shore from here?'

'I can try.'

'I'm going to take that as a yes. I want you to get me as close to the trigger wolf as you can.'

'Very well.'

Wellingtonia launched herself from the raft and paddled strenuously through the freezing water towards the bank. Shivering and dripping, she clambered ashore and began to gallop towards the city. As they approached, they could see frightened humans, bears, sheep and other creatures streaming out through a ragged hole in the city wall. And behind them, smashing its way through buildings as easily as a child tearing paper, was the trigger wolf, its monstrous paws crushing everything in its path.

'It seems to be moving in roughly a straight line,'

said Grace. 'You see that tower in the distance it's heading for?'

'Yes?'

'Take me to the top of it.'

Wellingtonia gritted her teeth and galloped with all her strength. Her huge hoofs thundered against the road.

Panicking inhabitants of Crumblechester streamed past them in a frenzied effort to escape the destruction – a pair of elderly bears in pyjamas, a family of springheeled newts, several young rabbits wearing football kits. Others had formed an impromptu defence force and were trying to drive the trigger wolf out. A big tough-looking stag was thrashing its huge antlers against one of the trigger wolf's ankles while a ring of exploding gnomes were detonating themselves around another. But none of these counter-attacks seemed to be having any effect on the rampaging beast whatsoever.

When they arrived at the tower, Wellingtonia kicked open the door and raced up the narrow stone staircase leading to its upper floors. At the very top, a door led out to a flat roof surrounded by a low wall. It gave a spectacular view of the city. The swathe of destruction wrought by the trigger wolf looked like a single strip mown down the middle of an overgrown lawn. Grace slid down from Wellingtonia's back and unsheathed Swickstipe. The awful howls of the trigger wolf blasted their ears. The creature was barely one street away from where they stood. She raced to the edge of the roof and waved her sword at the gigantic beast.

'Here, girl! Over here! Come on! Who's a good girl? Who's a good girl? You are! Yes, you are! Yes, you are!'

The trigger wolf's ears pricked. Its enormous head swivelled towards Grace, its two huge blue eyes wide with curiosity.

'That's it, girl! Here I am! Come on! Good little wolf! Come to your auntie Grace!'

'Auntie Grace?' said Wellingtonia.

'Be quiet,' said Grace. 'I know how to talk to dogs.' She resumed waving. 'Come on! Come on, girl! Over here!'

A savage snarl curled its black lips. With a low,

booming growl, it bounded over to the tower.

'This is where we find out if my plan works,' said Grace with a nervous laugh. 'I'm ninety-nine per cent certain it will. Well, maybe ninety-eight. I think I've finally discovered my style of using Swickstipe. And tell me, are you able to close your ears?'

Wellingtonia snorted. 'Can I what?'

'Close your ears to block out sound.'

'I'm a horse, not a camel.'

'But can you?'

With effort, Wellingtonia folded her long ears in on themselves. 'Like this?'

'Perfect.'

The bellow of the approaching trigger wolf filled the air. It thrust its immense snout towards Grace and sniffed with a sound like the roar of a jet engine.

Grace put on her helmet. She waved Swickstipe towards the beast and watched as it followed the sword curiously with its eyes. It opened its vast jaws, preparing to lunge.

Grace's heart lurched. Her ninety-eight per cent

certainty her plan would work had plummeted to forty-eight. No, now it was thirty-eight. No, actually more like eighteen ...

Once again, she wished James was here to help her. She'd tell him she was sorry for breaking his guitar.

With a grunt, she slammed down Swickstipe's hilt on to the low wall surrounding the roof. The sword began to vibrate rapidly and a loud note rang out, a low, rich tone that sounded like the chanting of a thousand monks in some underground cavern.

OWWWWWWWWWWWWW ...

Even with the helmet clamped over her ears, Grace found the note almost overpowering. She knew if she stopped concentrating for a second it would blot out her thoughts completely.

OWWWWWWWWWWWWW ...

The trigger wolf froze, its head cocked to one side, listening, wondering, its eyes slowly turning blank and black as a pair of cannonballs. The savage snarl on its face melted away and, with a burst of noise like the crackling of a huge fire, the creature began to shrink. Soon, the trigger wolf was once more the size of an ordinary cub. It gave a long yawn and curled up comfortably on the dusty road beside the tower.

The sword finally stopped vibrating. Grace returned it to its scabbard. Seeing its inscription earlier had finally made her realise what had happened at the end of her sword fight with Petronilla Saxifrage. The sword's note when struck had produced a hypnotic effect that had caused them both to lose consciousness. The inscription on its blade referred not just to the agonised cries of its victims but to the mesmerising note it produced when struck against a hard surface. It was this noise that the sound of the Calming Conch had reminded her of.

Wellingtonia unfolded her ears and gave a joyous whinny. 'You did it, child! You saved the city!' She cantered over to Grace's side. Grace stroked her nose and then threw her arms around Wellingtonia's neck, holding her tightly.

'I know! Happy days!'

There was a loud plopping sound as a wizened toad in a tiara leaped from the window of a neighbouring building and landed beside them on the roof of the tower.

'Mary!' cried Wellingtonia excitedly. 'You're here! Wasn't that sensational? The Fifteenth Grace did it! And both sides cooperated! There's no need for us to fight now! No more need for the Worthy War!'

Mary gave a sniff. 'I didn't catch exactly how she did it but it would appear the Fifteenth Grace performed her task adequately. However, I'm afraid the Worthy War goes on.'

'But why?' asked Grace. 'The People of the Day and the People of the Night can see there's no real difference between them. Everyone wants to just get on with their lives.'

'Do not blaspheme in my presence!' barked Mary. 'The People of the Day will forever be super-ior to the People of the Night! The Worthy War merely enters a new phase. While your team has been dealing with the trigger wolf, another group have successfully captured the People of the Night's own saviour.'

Grace felt her legs go weak. 'The People of the

Night have their own version of me? First I've heard of it.' She felt as if someone were trying to steal her glory. It was a horribly familiar sensation.

'Indeed,' said Mary, 'and you shall fight them to the death.'

Grace folded her arms. 'I don't think I will, actually.'

She was still folding her arms when two burly venom goblins grabbed her and carried her away.

15

Saviours

Shortly afterwards, Grace found herself in a forest clearing some miles out of Crumblechester.

She had been dumped in an undignified heap after an equally undignified journey tied to the back of one of the venom goblins' horses. The rope had been tight, the road bumpy and the horse, whose name was Shirley, foul-mouthed.

How could this happen now? After she had saved everyone? The People of the Day and the People of the Night had shown they could coexist peacefully. So what was the point of continuing their stupid war?

Grace clambered slowly to her feet and took in her surroundings. A great number of humans and animals were standing around her in a wide circle, separated from her by a waist-high rope dotted with bunting. It was as if they were at Flakebury Summer Fete, she thought, bemused, and everyone was waiting for her to give a demonstration of axe-throwing or falconry.

She spotted Wellingtonia in the crowd. Jonathan, too. Both were surrounded by guards with swords and spears drawn. Both animals had tense expressions. Jonathan waved his arm at her and received a painful poke in the ribs from one of his captors. She scanned the faces for Sarah Fairchild. There was no sign of her.

'If I could have everyone's attention … ?' called a voice. Mary Mugwort's.

Grace turned to see Mary squatting on a small wooden stage behind the rope barrier. It looked a hastily assembled affair, no more than a few crates strapped together. The bat Scarlett Moss was hovering beside her.

'Thank you for attending this most important

and historic occasion,' said Mary. Her voice was solemn but Grace could see a hint of a wry smile at the corner of her wide, lipless mouth. 'Rumours reach me that the trigger wolf attack on our glorious capital Crumblechester has united members of the People of the Day and the People of the Night in mutual aid and respect as they tried to save one another from the awful beast, and that all over our county citizens are putting aside their long-held enmities in the name of

friendship. Such
people, let me
make it entirely
clear, *are traitors!*'

'Hear, hear!' trilled Scarlett Moss.
'Traitors!'

'Our two Peoples must be forever separate, as different as the Day and Night after which we name ourselves,' continued Mary.

'But we recognise that our War, though Worthy, cannot go on indefinitely,' said Scarlett. 'Wars are expensive in terms of resources, in time and in the lives of our citizens. Something must be done to end the hostilities once and for all.'

'And the solution to this is not peace and

cooperative coexistence, as some wrongly think,' said Mary, 'but victory!'

'The outright victory of one of the two sides!' piped Scarlett.

'The complete domination of one People by the other,' said Mary.

'Therefore …' said Scarlett.

'Therefore …' said Mary.

'We have decreed …'

'After some wrangling …'

'That the final battle of the Worthy War should be a fight to the death between our two saviours!'

Grace's stomach lurched.

'It has been agreed,' said Mary, 'that the People of the winner of this fight shall be declared Supreme Rulers of Brokenshire.'

'And the losing side,' said Scarlett, 'shall become the Downtrodden Servants of Brokenshire, completely at the command of the Supreme Rulers.'

'One fight to settle everything.'

'Everything!'

'So it is agreed.'

'So it is agreed.'

'Not by me it isn't,' said Grace.

A venom goblin in the crowd raised a knobbly finger to its lips and shushed her.

'This final battle will take place here,' said Scarlett.

'In this ancient Brokenshire duelling ring,' said Mary. 'It is surrounded by a magic-retardant cord that will prevent our combatants receiving outside aid.'

In the crowd, a uniformed boar beat a rhythm loudly on a drum.

'People of the Day!' said Scarlett. 'Is your saviour ready to fight?'

'She is!' cried Mary.

Grace's veins seemed to clog with slush. 'Now hang on. I haven't actually agreed to anything here!' She hurriedly pulled down the visor of her helmet and drew Swickstipe from its scabbard. Was she really about to have a duel to the death? Unlucky neon tetra in the school aquarium aside, she couldn't *really* kill anyone or anything.

Could she?

Did she even have a choice?

'People of the Night!' exclaimed Mary. 'Is your saviour ready to fight?'

'He is!' shouted Scarlett.

Grace looked around, panic rising inside her. What would the People of the Night's saviour be? A savage dinosaur … ? A venom goblin … ? Some brutish badger knight … ?

The crowd parted and a figure ducked under the barrier to enter the arena. They were human in shape, tall, and wearing armour and a helmet not so very different from Grace's own. The figure drew a long sword and held it aloft. Ready.

Grace eyed the rope barrier and the ring of eager faces gazing at her, desperate for the slightest hint of a gap, for some clue as to how she might escape.

But there was nothing.

She was on her own.

As one, Mary and Scarlett exclaimed: 'Let the final battle of the Worthy War … *commence!*'

The armoured figure approached Grace without hurry, sword outstretched, taking their time to evaluate their opponent.

Grace backed away, her own weapon pointing at the figure. She cast a few quick glances around for a stone or even tree against which she could strike Swickstipe to produce its hypnotic note and potentially stun the other saviour, but could see nothing bigger than a tiny green shrub.

The figure made a sudden lunge at her with their sword. It wasn't particularly forceful – more of an experimental prod – but it made Grace leap backwards with a sudden spasm of fear.

A cheer went up in the crowd.

How did Mary expect her to defeat this other saviour? Surely the old toad knew that Grace was no expert sword fighter, even after her training session with Petronilla Saxifrage? Then she noticed that the other saviour seemed to be dragging their left leg as they walked. Limping, in fact, rather badly. *So that was it.* Mary thought even a novice like Grace stood a reasonable chance against an injured opponent.

It was all so cruel. So unfair …

SWISSSSHHHHH!

The other saviour's sword slashed through the air in front of Grace's nose. Injured or not, her opponent was apparently determined to go through with this duel.

She sidestepped and struck at the figure's armoured breastplate with her sword. The figure emitted a grunt and staggered back a few paces.

Buoyed by this tiny success, Grace advanced on her opponent. Perhaps she might not lose after all? Perhaps she need only injure the other saviour a bit? Put them sufficiently out of action so that Grace could be declared winner? Might not that be enough to end the fight?

CLANNNNNNNG!

The other saviour slammed the flat end of their sword against Grace's stomach like a cricket bat, smashing the air from her lungs. She hurtled backwards and fell heavily on to her back near the tiny green shrub, panting. Dazed.

Through the slits in her helmet visor she saw the grey-green non-sky of Brokenshire overhead. It was odd to think that there were fields and houses and rivers directly above her. She wondered if there was anyone up there now looking down at her.

Grace could hear the other saviour's footsteps

approaching. She tried to move. Couldn't. *Oh well.* So this was it. She'd had an interesting life. Mostly boring and normal and then with a crazy adventure stuck right on the very end. Quite short. She hadn't even finished reading all the Narnia books yet.

The helmeted face of the other saviour loomed into view. They raised their sword high.

Another cheer, this one ear-splittingly loud, burst from the crowd.

'Move, m'deario!' whispered a voice in Grace's ear. '*Move now or you'll regret it!*'

Grace turned her head. The shrub was talking to her! And she had recognised its voice.

'Sarah?'

'*Correct, m'deario! Went to a witch doctor and got my magic back, didn't I? Thought I'd disguise myself as this shrub in case you needed any assistance. The ring may keep magic out but it keeps it in too! But you don't need no magic now, trust me. Just move! And be quick about it!*'

With the final crumbs of her strength, Grace gritted her teeth and rolled on to her side – just as her opponent thrust their sword downwards. The blade went almost half its length into the soft earth, causing the other saviour to grunt in surprise. Grace swept out a foot and connected with the ankle of the other saviour's injured leg. The armoured figure roared in pain and tumbled to the ground.

Victory surged through Grace's veins. She hauled herself to her feet and raised Swickstipe high above the chest of her opponent, her heart pounding like the boar's drum. Where should she injure them? An arm? Another leg? What would *really* put them out of the fight for good?

'Finish them, Grace!' cried Mary from the crowd. 'It's the only way to ensure victory!'

Grace took a deep breath, considering …

'Grace? Is that actually you?'

'Hey? What?'

'Grace! It is you! I thought I recognised that backpack!'

The other saviour pulled off their helmet.

Time seemed to stop. Grace's eyes became saucer wide.

'Jaaaaames!' Her brother's name exploded out of her mouth in a scream of pure astonishment. She flung off her own helmet and helped him to his feet, then hugged him so tightly that their armour clanked together. 'I nearly ... you nearly ... we both ... I've been ... it's all just ...'

'So, you're a saviour too, are you?' said James, amused. 'It must run in the family.'

Grace nodded mutely. Her eyes were swimming with tears.

'Thanks for not, y'know, killing me with your sword,' said James.

Grace laughed and wiped her eyes with the heel of one gauntleted hand. 'Oh. No big deal.'

'What in Brokenshire is going on?' demanded Mary.

'Yes!' trilled Scarlett. 'This is not what we agreed!'

'Fight!' yelled Mary.

'To the death!' yelled Scarlett.

'I don't think so,' said James.

'This duel is over,' said Grace. 'And so should be your pathetic war.'

'But there must be conflict!' insisted Mary.

'We need enemies – winners and losers, all that

kind of thing,' demanded Scarlett. 'What is life without them?'

'Pretty sick, I reckon,' said Grace.

'But the prophecies!' said Mary.

'The prophecies must come to pass!' said Scarlett.

Grace took *The Holy History of Brokenshire* from her backpack and held it aloft. 'This thing is the cause of all your troubles,' she called to them. 'Why do you let it dominate your lives?'

'You've got one of those, too, have you?' said James. He opened a leather pouch hanging from a belt on his armour and drew out a similar book. 'The People of the Night's version has a white cover with a picture of Pertle the Pious Poet on it. Oh, and a different set of prophecies, I should think. Ones that suggest the People of the Night are the good guys and the People of the Day are the nasty ones.'

Grace and James exchanged books and flicked through them. Grace jabbed a finger at some text on the first page of James's *Holy History*.

'There,' she said. 'Can you find the same page in mine?'

James thumbed through the book. 'Yes. Got it.'

'And do you see what I see?'

James nodded. 'I do.'

On both pages of the books, in a small but elegant typeface, and set amid the familiar teardrop-shaped logo, were clearly printed the words:

Published by Dart-Hagger Books

'The prophecies of your so-called sacred song singer Soros and precious poet Pertle are both published by the same company,' called James to Mary and Scarlett.

'You might say that they're both the product of the same higher power,' said Grace.

A murmur of consternation rippled through the crowd.

'Who?' called someone.

'Yes, who?' called another.

'Who is behind the works of our great prophets?' called a third.

Grace closed James's copy of the *Holy History* and raised her eyebrows. 'Dart-Hagger's the tunnel at the very north of the county, isn't it? I say we go there and find out.'

'But it's forbidden to go there!' said Scarlett.

'The *Holy History* itself says so!' chipped in Mary. 'Space-time twists there in a most dangerous manner!'

'Either that,' said Grace, 'or someone really doesn't want you to visit the place.' She ran a finger over the large teardrop shape on its cover.

'It's like all the hatred and nastiness in the county pours out from that one spot,' said James.

'Or funnels *into* it!' cried Grace, her eyes lighting up. 'Blimey, what are we waiting for?'

She strode towards the edge of the ring, James following.

'Out of the way,' she bellowed confidently. 'Saviours coming through.'

16

The Business End

The skyless sky of Brokenshire shrank until it became a long dark tunnel of grey rock.

They were at the extreme north end of the county, heading for the pointed tip at the very apex of the teardrop shape. Grace and James led the party, striding ahead purposefully, their armour gleaming dully in the dim light. Next came Jonathan, Sarah (now back in human form), the two horses Wellingtonia and Olive Willow, with Mary Mugwort and Scarlett Moss at the rear and exchanging occasional scowls.

Ahead they could just make out the glitter of a large round silvery object.

'What's that?' asked Jonathan.

'Of course,' murmured Sarah. 'A psychic lens! About the biggest I ever saw! They told us all about these 'orrible things in magic school. Dark witches and wizards used them to consume enormous power in days gone by.'

'What does it do?' asked Grace. 'This one?'

'Put simply, m'dear, it's a hate funnel.'

James frowned. 'A what?'

Sarah pointed at the device. 'Through that opening it gathers all the negative psychic energy present in the air that's been generated by people's emotions. All the hate, nastiness, enmity, bad vibes and so on people feel during wartime.'

Grace wrinkled her nose. 'Yuck.'

Sarah nodded. 'Yuck indeed. It takes all this ill will that hangs in the air of our county like an invisible fog and funnels it into a concentrated stream of the purest, shining hatred. This distilled essence of hate is mighty rich in the dark magical energies that are like nectar to those accustomed to their blackly bitter taste. A diet of such energy can increase the lifespan of anyone who consumes it by hundreds of years.'

Grace felt suddenly cold. 'That's totally diabolical. What kind of monster would do something like that?'

Sarah smiled grimly. 'That's what we're here to find out, in't it?'

Grace felt like an ant crawling along the inside of an ice-cream cone. Ahead at the end of the narrowing tunnel lay a large silver funnel about as tall as a house. It glinted and glowed, almost alive. Agonised ghostly patterns flickered across its metallic surface, manifestations of the raw hatred coursing within.

'The psychic lens doesn't look terribly strong or defended in any way,' said Grace. 'I reckon it should be easy enough to break.'

'Especially when it's being attacked by a crazed T. rex,' said Jonathan.

'You don't seem very crazed to me,' said Grace.

'Give me time,' said Jonathan. 'Just thinking about all the senseless waste and death this thing has leeched from over the centuries is enough to put a crimp in anyone's mood.'

He took a step towards the funnel, his tail slowly

rippling like a huge snake about to strike.

'Intruders!' said a voice. 'I haven't encountered any intruders for years and years! I wouldn't be surprised if I'd completely forgotten how to kill them. How amusing! Oh, wait. Yes. I remember now.'

A tall figure hobbled into view around the edge of the funnel. It was a man, old in years but power-fully built with thick,

muscular arms and shoulders. He had long hair and a long beard that reached down to his stomach. The right half of his beard and hair was entirely white, while the left half was a glossy black. He wore a long robe decorated with black-and-white checks, giving him the appearance of a walking chessboard. In both hands, he held a gigantic sword almost as long as he was tall.

'Soros!' cried Mary. She was on the right of the tunnel and could see only the sides of his hair and beard that were white.

'Pertle!' cried Scarlett, who was on the left and could see only the black half of his hair and beard.

Soros-Pertle twisted to the left and right to show them his true colouring. 'Both, I think you'll find. It was necessary to create two scribes to maintain my little conceit. A simple *us versus them* opposition is always the best way to stir up hatred. It is a formula tried and tested over many centuries.'

The air crackled with energy. A bolt of fire flew from Sarah Fairchild's fingers towards Soros-Pertle. There was a bang as loud as a thunderclap as the black-and-white-clad figure swatted away the bolt with his enormous sword.

Soros-Pertle grinned at Sarah. 'I think you'll find this weapon of mine sufficient to ward off any spell.' He turned to Jonathan. 'To say nothing of being sharp enough to pierce the scales of a dinosaur. I do believe I shall rather enjoy myself killing you. Already I can feel your hatred for me flooding into my veins through the funnel. Ironic, is it not, that your own emotions shall fuel the flame that consumes you?'

He raised the sword.

'And this, my friends, is the end of you.'

Grace looked at James. Both nodded, raised their swords aloft and flung them with all their strength. Soros-Pertle watched, first with amusement and then with gathering horror, as the swords flew past him on either side and tore through the thin silvery sheet of the funnel. There was a terrible screaming sound. Blinding rays of energy flew from its silvery surface as the gleaming metal structure crumpled, ragged.

Soros-Pertle grunted and froze, limbs stiffening, his eyes wide with terror.

'All that lovely hate! Just evaporating away to nothingness. This is … *bad news*,' he croaked.

A crack appeared in the middle of his forehead. It spread quickly across his face, then down his neck and across his chest until its dark filaments crisscrossed his entire body.

Grace and the others exchanged bewildered glances.

There was a tiny *fring* – like the noise made by a dying light bulb – and Soros-Pertle shattered into thousands of tiny fragments, which pattered and tinkled on the stone floor of the tunnel.

Silence.

James grasped Grace's arm. 'Is that it? Is it over?'

Grace shook her head. 'Look! There!'

Among the shards of what had once been Soros-Pertle, something was moving, small and mouse-like. A tiny head emerged. It was connected to a tiny body. A small grey figure with fangs and pointed ears.

'Bless my soul,' breathed Sarah Fairchild. 'It's a venom goblin!'

'A very small one,' said Jonathan.

'And getting smaller all the time,' said Grace.

And this was true. The tiny figure was shrinking before their eyes. It bared its fangs at them and shook its tiny fists.

'Curses upon you!' it squeaked as it shrivelled. 'You shall rue the day you crossed Dart-Hagger! You shall feel my wrath and never again will you ...'

They couldn't hear what he said next, because he had vanished.

Grace and James retrieved their swords from the collapsed remains of the hate funnel.

James wiped his clean with his gauntlet. 'Good old Slangfash. You've served me well.'

'Your sword's called Slangfash?' said Grace. 'I love it!'

'What's yours called?' asked James.

'Swickstipe.'

'Yeah?' He nodded. 'Cool name.'

The next day, a meeting was held in the glittering conference room of the Governor's Palace in Crumblechester. Around a polished wooden table sat Grace, James, Mary Mugwort and Scarlett Moss.

Sitting on a row of species-friendly fancy chairs of various sizes that ran the perimeter of the room were Wellingtonia, Olive Willow, Jonathan Vetchling, Sarah Fairchild, Cardinal Axminster, a tall gangly man called Rowan Snipwell and a small fierce bird whom Grace heard referred to as Marwood the Storm-Robin.

Spread out on the wooden table was a large parchment, several columns of neat black ink still shiny and fresh on its clean white surface.

Grace looked over at Mary and Scarlett. 'All good, then, ladies? All agreed?'

The toad and the bat nodded, too.

'Indeed,' said Scarlett.

'Let's do this,' said Mary.

'Do all four of us sign the agreement?' asked James.

'Yes,' said Grace. 'Each of us has our own dotted line.'

'It would look nice,' said Scarlett, 'if we each signed our names in a different colour, wouldn't it? Sort of symbolic.'

'A pity we don't have four differently coloured inks,' said Mary.

'Actually,' said Grace. She rummaged in her

rucksack and pulled out her special four-coloured pen. 'I have just the thing. *Woop woop!*'

A tremendous feast took place after the signing ceremony in the square outside the palace. Jonathan Vetchling had been in charge of the catering and all who attended agreed that the food was some of the finest they had ever tasted, and many were pleasantly surprised to discover afterwards that all the ingredients had been vegan. Several suggested to Jonathan that he open his own bakery.

It was a joyous occasion. Ex-People of the Day partied with former People of the Night, but everyone now agreed that they were simply 'people'. The Worthy War that had dominated the lives of every single inhabitant of Brokenshire for so long lay exposed and dead for the awful lie it was. A new, peaceful dawn awaited. Exploding gnomes detonated with delight. Slate dragons gave rides to children. Dodos laughed until their bellies wobbled. And somewhere among the happy mass of revellers, a venom goblin far friendlier than the ill-fated Dart-Hagger received his first ever invitation to join a book group.

17

All the Fun

To Grace's delight, they were rebuilding the fairground.

The stinking soot and ash had been hosed away and a band of workers were busily recreating Rocky Stark's Far-Out Fun Plaza, hammering nails into boards and painting signs in cheerful colours. A couple of badgers were attaching an awning to a stall that would sell something called Sugared Bog-Floss.

Grace and James were standing outside the shed. They had walked here from Crumblechester together and had plenty of time to talk on the way.

They had never talked much before, each wrapped up in their own lives and opinions, and each twin had learned a lot about the other. James, for instance, had a phobia about needles (*why had Grace never known this?*) and Grace's favourite type of dog was a border collie. James hadn't even realised that Grace *had* a favourite type of dog.

There was one subject, however, that Grace hadn't dared raise and now, with the prospect of return to their home imminent, she felt it could no longer be avoided.

'James.'

'Yes?'

'I broke your guitar.'

'What?'

'Stood on it. Smashed it. It's ruined.'

'Ruined?'

'I didn't mean to. I thought it was your sports bag. I stood on it to reach a book off a shelf. Put my foot right through it. I know what it means to you, that guitar. I really am incredibly sorry.'

James shrugged. 'OK. Forget it.'

'What?'

'You heard me. Don't worry about it.'

Grace spluttered. 'Don't worry about it? I was so flipping worried about it I went off on a bizarre magical quest, mate!'

'Well, it's fine now. Really.'

'How can you be so calm about it?'

'It sort of serves me right, really.'

Grace blinked. 'How? How does my smashing your guitar serve you right? What did you do?'

James looked away. He smiled weakly. 'I sort of tried to kill you.'

'You *what*?'

He held up his hands. 'I didn't *know* it was you, obviously! I'd only just arrived here and Scarlett Moss told me you were a sworn enemy of the People of the Night. You were just a tiny speck on a horse in the distance, so I—'

'It was you,' said Grace, her eyes widening. 'You

knocked over the big wheel here when Wellingtonia and I first arrived!'

He nodded sheepishly. 'Like I say, I had no idea it was you. I thought I was doing my bit for the Worthy War, so ...'

'Forget it,' said Grace.

'Really?'

'Really.'

'No big deal?'

'No big deal.'

'We're cool?'

'As cucumbers.'

'How's the leg, by the way?'

'Much better, thanks. Someone put some blue gunk on it and it doesn't hurt so badly.'

Grace placed a gauntlet on the handle of the shed's door. 'Time to make tracks, I guess. I wonder how the other Grace is getting on at home.'

'And the other James.'

'What's your double like?'

'Nice guy, I thought,' said James. 'Bit of a panicker.'

'Mine too,' said Grace. 'Interesting girl, though.

Weird to think of all the battles and stuff they must have been through.'

'They're probably enjoying the rest.'

Grace grinned devilishly. 'Maybe we should leave them to it for a bit longer?'

James laughed. 'Maybe we should.'

'They've finished rebuilding the big wheel here and they're looking for volunteers to try it out. Shall we?'

'Rude not to.'

They turned from the shed and strode back into the fairground. The smell of new paint was everywhere.

THE END

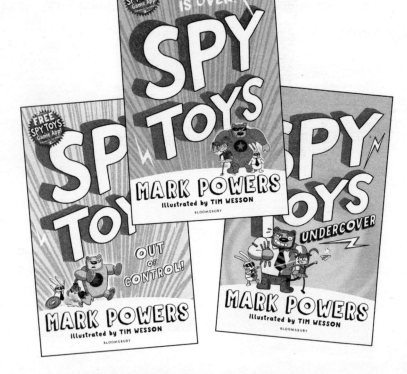

LOOK OUT FOR

About the Author

Mark Powers has been making up ridiculous stories since primary school and is slightly shocked to find people now pay him to do it. He grew up in North Wales and now lives in Manchester. His favourite animals are the binturong, the aye-aye and the dodo.

About the Illustrator

Coralie Muce is a French illustrator and concept artist who grew up in Paris and graduated from the Émile Cohl School of Art in Lyon. She is inspired by absurd stories like *Alice in Wonderland* and loves drawing witches. She is very fond of pigeons and always shares her picnic with them.